"Why did you come running home, Laurel?

You're back in town, making me want you until I ache, making me relive all the memories of what we shared, and you're keeping so many damn secrets it's a wonder you can even function."

"I..."

"Well, I know one truth about you, Laurel Windsong," Ben said, a rough edge to his voice as he gripped her shoulders. "When I kissed you by the lake, you responded to me, totally, absolutely, holding nothing back. You desire me as much as I do you. And that is a fact. There's no secret about it, Laurel."

And with that, Ben pulled her close and captured her mouth with his in a searing kiss.

A WEDDING IN WILLOW VALLEY

JOAN ELLIOTT PICKART

SPECIAL EDITION

Published by Silhouette Books

America's Publisher of Contemporary Romance

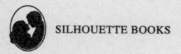

SILHOUETTE BOOKS

ISBN 0-373-24754-0

A WEDDING IN WILLOW VALLEY

Books by Joan Elliott Pickart

JOAN ELLIOTT PICKART

is the author of over one hundred books. When she isn't writing, Joan enjoys reading, needlework, gardening and attending craft shows on the town square. She has all-grown-up daughters, as well as a young daughter, Autumn, who is in elementary school. Joan, Autumn and a five-pound poodle named Willow live in a charming small town in the high pine country of Arizona.

For Phyllis
Good friend, good neighbor
and
the best cookie-baker
in the west!

slowly. And then she arrived unannounced in Willow Valley, stepped behind the counter at the Windsong Café with an order pad in her hand and acted as though she had never left in the first place. He'd been flung back in time and felt raw and wounded again as well as exhausted from lack of sleep.

He'd been doing his best to avoid Laurel, and when he saw her, he didn't look directly into those incredible dark eyes of hers. He had nothing he wanted to say to her because it had all been said ten years before. He just wanted her to pack up and leave again, get out of Willow Valley and not come back.

Because while she was here, there was nowhere for him to hide from the truth that was ripping him to shreds.

He was still in love with Laurel Windsong.

Ben smacked the steering wheel with the heel of one hand and clenched his jaw so tightly his teeth ached.

He'd arrest Laurel for disturbing his peace of mind, he thought. He'd toss her in jail, tell her she had twenty-four hours to get out of town or he'd throw away the key to the cell.

"There you go, Skeeter," he muttered as he shook his head. "That's really mature, rational thinking."

Ben reached the edge of town, turned around and drove back, his practiced eye sweeping over all for any sign of trouble brewing.

There were a lot of strangers in town already this Saturday, and no doubt more were on the way to see the autumn leaves. It was good for the business owners. It was constant vigilance for him and his deputies.

The tourists kept him very busy, and to top it off he was dealing with a rash of break-ins at the presently unoccupied summer homes. Carefully selected houses had been targeted, and the knot in his gut told him that meant it was someone from Willow Valley or the reservation at the edge of town pulling off those robberies.

There were a thousand people living in Willow Valley and the same number on the rez. Somewhere in the midst of them, someone had turned on his own people—and that made Ben rip-roaring angry.

Ben's stomach rumbled, and a quick look at his watch told him it was lunchtime.

Maybe he'd go home and see what he could throw together for a meal, he mused. Or get some fast food that would sit like a brick in his stomach the rest of the afternoon. He could settle for some of those dinky sandwiches that didn't even have any crust on them at the bed-and-breakfast.

No, damn it, he wanted a good-tasting, nourishing lunch, and the best place to get that was the Windsong Café. He'd just ignore Ms. Laurel Windsong, as he usually did when he ate there, and enjoy the food. Fine. That's how he'd handled her being back since she'd popped into town, and he would keep right on doing it.

No problem.

As long as he didn't look at her too long.

As long as he didn't envision freeing her silken hair from that long braid she wore by drawing his fingers through it and watching it slide over his hands like an ebony waterfall.

As long as he didn't relive the exquisite memories of making love with Laurel and hearing her whisper his name and declare her love for him.

As long as he ignored the fact that she'd stolen his heart many, many years ago and he didn't have a clue as to how to get it back.

Ben pulled into a parking place down the block from the café, radioed in that he was going to lunch but would be carrying his handheld if he was needed, then grabbed his tan Stetson that matched the rest of his uniform from the passenger seat of the patrol car.

A few moments later he was striding toward the Windsong Café, a muscle ticking in his tightly clenched jaw.

Laurel frowned as Ben Skeeter entered the café. She turned immediately to see if any of her orders were ready to be picked up, despite the fact she'd done that two seconds before.

Darn the man, she thought. Doesn't he ever have any leftovers in his refrigerator at home he could eat for lunch? Or get an urge for fast food, like the rest of the population? Oh, no, not Ben. He had to show up here at the Windsong Café day after day and cause her heart to race and memories to assault her.

Ben. Oh, Ben, Laurel thought, still not moving. There was a time when they had shared everything— hopes, dreams, secrets, plans for the future, their hearts, minds, bodies, the very essence of who they were. They'd been so much in love, so connected that they'd envisioned themselves as one entity.

But that was then, and this was now, and since she'd arrived back in Willow Valley they'd attempted to avoid each other. When they did meet, they were polite, exchanged brief greetings, but never made eye contact. They were strangers now, separated by ten years and shattered dreams. She would continue to keep her distance from Ben just as she'd done since she'd come home.

There was just one thing wrong with that grand plan, she thought dismally.

She was still deeply in love with Benjamin Skeeter.

* * *

Ben sat in the first booth and swept his gaze over the café. It had the same motif as it had when Jimmy and Jane Windsong had opened for business years before. It had red vinyl booths along the front to afford a view out the windows, stools at the counter and wooden tables in the space beyond. An old-fashioned jukebox was against the far wall, and plastic-coated menus were nestled between metal napkin holders and the salt and pepper shakers.

It wasn't fancy. Never had been. But it was homey, inviting. The food was down-home cooking—hamburgers and fries served in red plastic baskets, meat loaf with mashed potatoes and gravy, chili and corn bread, pot roast and vegetables and other offerings that a person might have enjoyed at their mother's or grandmother's table.

Lush plants hung in woven baskets suspended from the ceiling by nearly invisible wires. The wall where the jukebox stood also boasted an enormous corkboard where pictures drawn by children were held in place by pushpins. Visitors as well as local kids were invited to add to the ever-changing display, and crayons and paper were available on the tables.

"Hey, Sheriff," someone called.

"Hey, Cadillac. What brings you into town?"

"I need me some feed for my goats," Cadillac said from where he sat on a stool at the counter. "Figure I'll have me some of Missy Windsong's meat loaf while I'm here."

"Good thinking," Ben said. "Things quiet on the rez?"

Cadillac shrugged and turned back to his lunch, and Ben knew that was the end of the conversation. When Navajos were done talking, they were done. Where they stopped speaking in an interchange didn't always make sense, but that was just the way it was. Always had been, always would be.

Good ole Cadillac, Ben mused. No one knew his age, and his weathered face said he could be anywhere between forty and sixty. Whatever his last name was, it had been so long since it had been used he doubted anyone remembered what it was, maybe even Cadillac himself.

He was a little slow in the thinking department and loved gossip more than breathing, it seemed. But he had a heart of gold, would give a man the shirt off his back if he figured that guy needed it more than he did.

"Lunch?"

Ben glanced up to see Laurel standing next to the table with a pad and pencil in her hands.

"Hamburger, fries, coffee," Ben said, shifting his gaze to the tabletop. "Please."

Laurel wrote on the pad, spun around and hurried away.

There were, Ben thought, about ten people staring at him at this point to see if this was the day that more than a lunch choice would be communicated between him and Laurel Windsong. Ever since she'd come home, people who knew Ben and Laurel's history had been watching and waiting for something—anything—to happen between them.

But nothing ever did.

And nothing ever would.

What they'd had together was over, long gone, smashed to smithereens the day that Laurel left Willow Valley for Virginia. Why she was back all of a sudden, he didn't know, but it had nothing to do with him. She'd stopped loving him ten years before, and maybe someday he'd figure out how in the hell to stop loving her.

Laurel clipped the paper with Ben's order onto the revolving metal circle at the top of the pass-through window between the kitchen and the main section of the café.

Darn, darn, darn, she fumed as she refilled Cadillac's coffee mug. It had happened again. Just because she'd asked Ben Skeeter what he wanted for lunch, just because she had been so close to him, could smell that unique fresh-air aroma of his, see the thick black hair she used to run her fingers through when they... Just because Ben existed, for crying out loud, her heart had gone crazy and her hands had trembled slightly when she'd clipped the order slip into place.

Ben was tall for a Navajo, she mused, just over six feet, and filled out that uniform to perfection, the tan material accentuating his tawny skin and dark hair. His chiseled features with high cheekbones, straight blade of a nose and oh-so-kissable lips were a study in masculinity personified.

This had to stop, Laurel thought. If Ben ever became aware of the reaction she still had to being in close proximity to him, she'd be totally mortified. Being near her certainly didn't bother him, that was for sure. Granted, he didn't meet her gaze, but that was because he still hated her for leaving Willow Valley ten years ago.

His voice was flat when he spoke to her, even sounded rather bored when he ordered his lunch, and he didn't bother with the simplest social questions of how she was doing, or her opinion of the weather.

No, she was nothing more to Ben Skeeter than a bad memory. If it wasn't for the fact that he truly enjoyed the food at the Windsong Café he probably wouldn't even come in there. Ten years had thoroughly erased any feelings he had for her.

A woman in her early thirties entered the café and called a greeting to Laurel, bringing her from her tangled thoughts. The attractive woman took the booth in front of Ben's and scrutinized the menu as Laurel came around the counter, zoomed past Ben without a glance and stopped at the second booth.

"Hi, Marilyn," Laurel said. "It's so nice to see you. How's business at the beauty shop?"

"Busy, busy," Marilyn said. "My feet are killing me already and it's only lunchtime. I decided to have a Windsong special to fortify myself for the afternoon instead of the yogurt I brought from home." She looked at the menu again. "Mmm. What do I want? Here we go. A BLT on whole-wheat toast and a glass of milk. Oh, dear, don't tell me that May baked some goodies."

Laurel smiled. "Okay, I won't inform you that May made fresh cherry pie, pumpkin with whipped cream and an apple cobbler to die for. Those words will not pass my sealed lips."

"You're cruel," Marilyn said, laughing. "I haven't been able to resist May's cobbler since I moved here, as evidenced by the width of my hips. I'll have some, of course."

"Got it," Laurel said, writing on the pad. "And there's nothing wrong with the width of your hips, Ms. Montgomery." She paused. "Marilyn, I'm trying to decide if I should cut my hair."

"No." Ben said sharply, before he was even aware that he had spoken.

Laurel's head snapped around to stare at Ben in shock at the same moment that Marilyn shifted in the booth to look at him, and Cadillac spun on his stool with the same intention. Jane Windsong was just placing Ben's order in its red plastic basket on the pass-through ledge, and her hand halted in midair. Three other men next to Cadillac at the counter dipped their heads to steal a peek at Sheriff Skeeter.

"Oh? You don't think Laurel should cut her hair, Ben?" Marilyn said, a delighted twinkle dancing in her eyes.

A trickle of sweat ran down Ben's chest, and he immediately thought of ten places he'd rather be than sitting in that booth in the Windsong Café with half the world staring at him and waiting eagerly for his answer.

"Well…um…" he said. "Laurel is very visible here at the café because she works out front, not in the kitchen. Visitors expect to see Native Americans when they come to Willow Valley, and her hair…contributes…to the…um…image. I was simply reacting to what she said from a…practical, business standpoint."

"Ah," Marilyn said, then faked a cough to cover a burst of laughter as she turned back around in the booth.

"Why don't I believe that?" Cadillac mumbled, shaking his head.

"That young man's nose is going to grow," Jane said under her breath, finally placing the red basket on the ledge. "Laurel," she called, "Ben's order is up."

"Dandy," Laurel said, stomping over to get it. She brought it to Ben's table and plunked it in front of him. "Here. I'll get your coffee."

"Thanks," Ben said, reaching for a napkin.

Laurel left, then returned with a mug and the coffeepot, bending over slightly as she filled Ben's mug.

"What on earth is your problem?" she whispered. "You just embarrassed me to death, Ben Skeeter. My hair is none of your concern."

"I didn't mean to speak out loud," he said, his voice hushed. "I was as surprised as you were that I said…" He snatched up the ketchup bottle that was at the end of the table, took off the lid and shook the bottle over the fries. "You're not really considering cutting your hair, are you, Laurel?"

"Maybe," Laurel said, lifting her chin. "Maybe not. I haven't decided yet."

"Don't do it, Laurel," Ben said, looking directly into her dark eyes. "Your hair is so beautiful, so silky and… I remember how it felt when I…" He cleared his throat and switched his gaze to his lunch. "Aw, hell, I just dumped half a bottle of ketchup on these fries."

Laurel opened her mouth to say something snappy regarding adding an extra charge to Ben's bill for the extravagant use of the ketchup, but immediately realized she had absolutely no air in her lungs to let her speak.

She rushed behind the counter, put the coffeepot back where it belonged, then was amazed that she remembered to clip Marilyn's order into place. When she turned again, Cadillac and the three men next to him were all grinning at her.

"What!" she said none too quietly.

"Gotta go get me some goat feed," Cadillac said, sliding off his stool.

"Me, too," the man next to him said.

"You don't got no goats, Billy," Cadillac said.

"Oh," Billy said. "I'll watch you buy feed for yours, then."

"'Kay," Cadillac said, dropping some money on the counter.

The other two men decided quickly that they'd tag along for the inspiring trip of watching Cadillac buy goat feed. None of them waited for their change or looked at Sheriff Skeeter as they beat a very hasty retreat from the Windsong Café.

Ben sighed and began to scrape some of the ketchup off his fries with a fork. The bottom of the hamburger bun was now soaked with ketchup, so he resorted to eating the demolished meal with a knife and fork rather than attempt to pick up the burger.

If it wasn't for the fact that he was really hungry, Ben thought, he'd hightail it out of here. Man, what a jerk he'd made of himself. He had just engaged in the first one-on-one conversation he'd had with Laurel since she'd returned to Willow Valley and he'd come across as a complete idiot.

But, man, the mere image in his mind of Laurel cutting off that gorgeous silky hair of hers had rattled him. His drill-sergeant sounding "No" had popped right out of his mouth and... Oh, jeez.

Then Laurel had bent over and whispered at him, fury radiating in those fathomless dark eyes of hers. She wore the same light floral cologne she'd always used, and when she'd looked directly into his eyes it had taken every bit of willpower he had not to slide his hand to the back of her neck, bring her lips to his and...

Ben shifted in the booth as heat rocketed through his body, and he looked around quickly to be certain no one was watching him.

Cadillac and his cronies were no doubt down at the feed store, he thought dismally, relating what had happened at the Windsong Café between the sheriff and Laurel and cackling with pleasure to be the ones to spread the gossip. The tourists in the café had no idea what had transpired. But the locals? He didn't even want to think about it.

Ben finished what he could salvage of his lunch, placed money on the table then picked up his Stetson and his handheld from next to him in the booth. He slid out, turned and bumped squarely into Laurel, who was carrying Marilyn's lunch. He gripped one of Laurel's shoulders with his free hand to steady her.

"I'm sorry," he said, not releasing his hold on her. "I didn't see you there. Did anything spill? No, it looks fine." He nodded. "Good. Okay."

"May I pass, please?" Laurel said, looking at a button in the middle of Ben's shirt.

"In a minute," he said, his hand still on her shoulder. "I'm sorry I embarrassed you about the hair-cutting business. I was way out of line."

"Yes, you were, Sheriff Skeeter. Marilyn is waiting for her lunch."

Ben placed his Stetson on his head, the handheld under his arm, took the plate and glass of milk from Laurel, then turned and delivered them to a startled Marilyn.

"Enjoy your lunch," Ben said, then went back to where a stunned Laurel was still standing. "Do you or do you not accept my apology for speaking out of turn about you cutting your hair?"

"No, I don't," Laurel said, planting her hands on

her hips, "because Cadillac and his buddies are going to have a field day with what happened in here. The whole thing is going to be blown way out of proportion by the time it gets passed from person to person."

"Well, yeah, but…"

"And to add to the mix," Laurel continued, "if I cut my hair, it will appear that I'm throwing a tantrum because you said I shouldn't. If I don't cut it, it will be perceived that Laurel Windsong is doing what Ben Skeeter told her to, obedient thing that she is."

Ben grimaced.

"I could take a couple inches off your hair, Laurel," Marilyn said from where she was sitting. "That might muddle the minds of the general populace of locals. You got a haircut, sort of, but then again, you didn't. So? How's that?"

"I'll give it some thought," Laurel said.

"Eat your lunch, Marilyn," Ben said, frowning.

Marilyn laughed. "You're getting crabby, Ben Skeeter. You're the one who caused this whole fiasco. I'm just trying to be helpful."

Ben's handheld squawked, and he nearly hugged it for ending the conversation.

"Gotta go," he said. "See ya."

As Ben hurried out the door, Laurel watched him go, then began to clear the dishes from the booth where he'd been sitting.

"Well, it took four months or so, Laurel," Marilyn said, "but you and Ben finally said more than three or four words to each other. Interesting. Very interesting."

"Eat your lunch, Marilyn," Laurel snapped, which caused the owner of the beauty shop to dissolve in laughter.

To Laurel's amazement, the following hours went quickly and she was actually able to blank her mind due to the fact that they were extremely busy at the café. She and the other two waitresses hustled back and forth. Jane and her assistants in the kitchen never stopped preparing meals as well as afternoon snacks of May's homemade pastries.

During the lull before the dinner crowd began to appear all the tables and the counter were given a scrubbing, the floor was swept, salt and pepper shakers filled, and on and on.

It was only when Laurel had to replace the ketchup bottle that Ben had nearly emptied onto his lunch that the entire episode began to replay, frame by frame, in her mind.

Ben didn't want her to cut her hair, she mused as she checked the supply of napkins in the metal holders. He'd even said that her hair was beautiful and that he could remember how it had felt when...

Laurel sank onto a stool at the counter, plunked

her elbow on top and rested her chin in her palm as she stared into space.

Goodness, she thought, this was so confusing. Why should Ben care one way or another what she did with her hair? And why had he been able to remember so quickly how it had felt when... This didn't make sense at all. Ben Skeeter despised her, saw her as the person who had broken his heart by breaking her promises. So why...

"You look deep in thought," Jane said, sliding onto the stool next to her daughter. "We've been so busy we haven't had a second to talk all day. Are you all right after your...encounter, shall we say, with Ben?"

Laurel sighed. "I guess so. The whole thing was...confusing. That's the word my mind keeps coming back to because it describes it the best. Confusing." She paused. "Thank goodness that the majority of the customers today were tourists and I didn't have to deal with the locals staring at me like a bug under a microscope."

"That will come," Jane said, laughing. "People have been watching you and Ben ever since you came home, and something finally happened between the two of you. Ben Skeeter definitely does not want Laurel Windsong to cut her hair. I imagine that news flash has been delivered through town and out to the rez by now."

"Great," Laurel said glumly. "What would we do without Cadillac? We have him, so we ought to do away with telephones."

"All you can do is hope some fresh gossip comes along very quickly," Jane said. "Like…oh, I don't know…someone robs the bank."

"Not going to happen," Laurel said.

"Nope," Jane said. "You're just going to have to grin and bear this until people get tired of talking about it." She stared into space. "You could have knocked me over with a feather when Ben hollered that you were not to cut your hair. That man certainly has a strong opinion on the subject, doesn't he?"

"Mother," Laurel said, sitting up straight on the stool, "you're doing what everyone else is doing by now. You're speculating about what happened and enjoying every minute of it. Shame on you. Where is your loyalty to your only child?"

"Well, honey," Jane said, smiling, "you must admit it was quite a show."

"It was a confusing show, that's what it was," Laurel said, sliding off the stool. "And I don't wish to discuss it further, thank you very much."

"Yes, dear. I understand," Jane said. "Well, I'm going home for a while and put my feet up before it's time for the dinner crowd. Everything is under control here. Do you want to come with me?"

"No, I feel edgy, restless," Laurel said. "I think I'll go for a walk and—oh, that's brilliant. If I stroll down the sidewalk, everyone will pounce on me. Yes, Mother, I'll drive home with you. And once I get there, I'm going to hide in my closet."

Chapter Two

At the small house where Jane and Jimmy Windsong had lived during their entire marriage, Jane decided to walk down the block and check on an elderly woman neighbor who had been a bit under the weather.

Laurel wandered into her bedroom, slipped off her shoes and stretched out on the bed, hoping to take a nap for no other reason than it would give her a reprieve from replaying in her mind yet again what had happened with Ben at the café.

After staring at the ceiling for fifteen minutes, she sighed, gave up the attempt and sat up on the edge of the bed to look out the window facing the tiny backyard. A playful breeze chased a colorful autumn leaf across the expanse, swirled it around then picked it up and carried it away to yet unknown adventures.

Ten years ago, Laurel thought, she had been like that leaf. She'd left the familiar, this bedroom in the home where she'd grown up, the charming town of Willow Valley, her mother, friends and…and Ben. She'd traveled across the country to Virginia to attend the college that had awarded her a scholarship, obtained her degree then begun her career as a high school psychologist.

She'd been brimming with optimism and enthusiasm, had been convinced that she was going to accomplish great things, help the troubled youths entrusted to her care, make a difference in their lives. She would unravel their confusion, untangle their problems, bring smiles to the frowning faces of those who sought her out.

Laurel shook her head and wrapped her hands around her elbows as she continued to stare out the window.

Such lofty dreams and goals she'd had, she thought. She'd ignored the yearning for those she loved in Willow Valley, the chilling homesickness that had woken her in the night to stare into the darkness, feeling so alone.

The lack of money had not allowed her to come

home often during the years she was away. But when she had returned for visits, she'd savored every moment, wrapped the memories of her time here around her like a warm, comforting blanket. She'd spent hours with her best friend, Dove Clearwater, talked long into the night with her mother, gone for walks among the tall pine trees with Grandfather, listening intently to every word of his quietly spoken wisdom.

But she hadn't spoken to Ben Skeeter.

They had not had a private conversation in over ten years…until today at the Windsong Café.

Ten years, Laurel mused, watching a squirrel chattering to another one in the backyard. Ten years had gone by, and here she sat in the bedroom of her youth, having come—no, *run*—home four months ago to seek solace like a trembling child in the arms of her mother. Jane Windsong was the only person in Willow Valley who knew what had happened in Virginia.

She hadn't even told Dove or Grandfather why she had returned so suddenly. But because they cherished the ways of the Dinet, the People, the Navajos, neither would pressure her for an explanation. Their beliefs stated that if they asked her the question four times, she was honor-bound to tell the truth, but neither would do that. She was so grateful for that, because she just couldn't bear to tell them that she had… No.

Laurel got to her feet.

She was thinking too much again, she admonished herself, dwelling on things that couldn't be changed and depressing herself. She had to quit this pity-party nonsense she kept indulging in, start distancing herself emotionally from what had taken place in Virginia and move forward with her life.

Forward? Toward what? she thought as she walked across the small room. To a future working side by side with her mother at the Windsong Café? Her mother seemed perfectly happy with her existence as it was, but…

"Oh, stop thinking, Laurel Windsong," she said aloud, with a cluck of self-disgust. "Just turn off your mind and shut up."

She went down the short hallway, through the medium size living room and on to the kitchen, where she found her mother sitting at the table with a cup of tea and the evening newspaper.

"Hi," Laurel said. "How's Mrs. Henderson feeling?"

Jane smiled. "She was on her way out the door to play canasta. Claimed she was as good as new."

"Well, that's fine," Laurel said, sitting down opposite her mother. "May I ask you something?"

Jane set the newspaper aside. "Of course."

"Dad died when I was sixteen," Laurel said.

"During all these years you've been alone have you ever considered the possibility of marrying again? You're only forty-six years old, Mother, which means you're facing many, many years yet on your own. Wouldn't you like someone to share your life with?"

"My goodness," Jane said. "Where is this subject coming from?"

"Oh, I don't know. I try to envision my own future and it's just a foggy mess. Then my mind bounces around and I think about you. I was just wondering if you're as happy and contented with your existence as you appear to be."

Jane laughed. "Ah, my daughter the psychologist is attempting to delve into my mind. Well, good luck with that, my sweet girl. But to answer your questions… Yes, I am very contented and happy. As far as marrying again? No. That will never happen.

"Jimmy Windsong won my heart when I was fifteen years old, Laurel, and he still possesses it even though he isn't here with me. He's the only man I have ever—will ever—love. I married him at eighteen, had you at nineteen, started the Windsong Café with him and there I'll be until I'm old and creaky.

"The love I shared with your father was so rare and beautiful, Laurel. It was a once-in-a-lifetime thing, and I'd never have anything like it again. Since I'm not willing to settle for less, I have no intention of ever remarrying. I believed that you and Ben had that same kind of love, but... Oh, I'm sorry. I shouldn't have said that. It was very insensitive on my part."

"That's all right," Laurel said quietly. "I thought Ben and I had something special, too, but I was wrong. I wanted to go to college, but he refused to understand that, to wait for me.

"You know what happened. He gave me an ultimatum. Stay here in Willow Valley while he went to the police academy in Phoenix, then marry him when he returned or we were done, finished, over. And that was that. Laurel Windsong and Ben Skeeter did not have the kind of love that Jane Nelson and Jimmy Windsong did. Not even close."

"Oh, I'm not sure about that," Jane said.

"Mother, facts are facts. I was determined to go to college and Ben... Never mind. I keep doing this. I keep dwelling on the past and I'm driving myself crazy. It's my future I should be thinking about. What on earth am I going to do with my life? Please don't take offense, but I don't see myself being fulfilled by working with you at the café year after year after year."

"Of course you don't," Jane said. "That café wasn't your dream, it was your father's and mine. You're just stopping off there at the moment until you get things settled in your mind. You're still healing from what happened in Virginia, Laurel. Be patient. Be kind to yourself. Take one day at a time for now and wait for the inner peace to start to blossom within you. It will come."

"Maybe," Laurel said. "I certainly haven't made any progress with that since I came back to Willow Valley. I'm way overdue to stop feeling sorry for myself, dwelling on what happened. Let's change the subject. Was there anything interesting in the newspaper?"

"Dove wrote a lovely article about the autumn leaves we're enjoying and how they never fail to appear each year like a promise from nature that is always kept. Our Dove is such a talented writer."

"Yes," Laurel said, nodding. "Yes, she really is. I also think the rugs, blankets, shawls and what have you that she weaves on her loom are the most gorgeous ones in the shops here. They certainly sell well."

"Indeed they do," Jane said, then drained her cup. "Oh, there was a short paragraph regarding the fact that there was another robbery in one of the summer homes. Whoever is doing this knows exactly which houses are not lived in year-round. That indicates it's someone who lives in Willow Valley or on the rez. That's rather chilling when you think about it. It's one of our own."

Laurel frowned and nodded.

"Ben was quoted as saying," Jane continued, "that he and his deputies will be increasing the patrols around those homes and that he won't rest until the person—or persons—are apprehended." She paused. "So tell me, Laurel Jane Windsong, are you going to cut that gorgeous hair of yours or not?"

Laurel shrugged. "I don't know. It's all the way to my waist when it isn't braided. I don't think a single thick braid worn day after day is very sophisticated for someone of twenty-seven."

"It is," Jane said, smiling, "if you're half Navajo. You have Jimmy's hair, tawny skin tone and those dark, dark eyes. If it wasn't for your features being a bit delicate and your being tall and slender, there wouldn't be any evidence that I had a part in creating you. But anyway, it's your hair and you should do what pleases you."

"Oh? The whole town probably knows by now that Ben Skeeter doesn't feel that way about my hair. The nerve of that man to... Oh, don't get me started."

"I think that scene in the café was rather sweet," Jane said.

"Oh, spare me," Laurel said, getting to her feet. "I'm going to go freshen up so I'll be ready to head back to work."

Jane watched her daughter leave the room, marveling yet again at her beauty.

"Oh, Jimmy," she whispered, "our baby girl is so troubled, so unhappy, and I don't know what to do to help her."

As a breathtaking sunset streaked across the sky, Ben strolled along the sidewalk of the main street of town, his last self-appointed duty before ending his shift for the day.

Seven local citizens so far had asked him if he planned to eat dinner at the Windsong Café, something he very rarely did, preferring to prepare something for himself at home after a busy day. He'd also received some smug smiles and raised eyebrows from half a dozen of the shop owners who had made it a point to come to the door of their stores as he'd gone by on his patrol.

Oh, yeah, he thought, the story of the ridiculous scene with Laurel regarding whether or not she should cut her hair had definitely spread like wildfire. There was nothing he could do but say nothing and wait it out until the next bit of juicy gossip took its place.

Ben slowed his step even more as he went past the old-fashioned ice cream parlor.

Man, oh, man, he thought, he and Laurel had spent countless hours in that place eating hot-fudge sundaes and talking about their plans for the future.

They had been so young, so sure that everything would go just the way they were laying it out, their hopes and dreams connecting like a jigsaw puzzle that created a fantastic picture.

But then Laurel had decided she wanted more than he could offer, more than his love and the life they were to share in Willow Valley after they were married. Everything had fallen apart as though an invisible hand had reached out and flung the pieces of the puzzle into oblivion.

In the years after she left he'd tried to make a new puzzle, but there were always pieces missing. It was never truly whole again without Laurel in his life. He had learned to go on as things were, slowly but surely, but now Laurel was back and...

Ben stopped suddenly as he looked down to see a boy about five years old staring up at him with wide eyes.

"Hi," Ben said. "Where's your mom, kiddo?"

"In that store," the boy said, pointing to the one next to the ice cream parlor. "Are you a real Indian?"

Ben nodded. "Yep. I'm a Navajo."

"Wow. Is that a real gun?"

"Yep."

"Wow. How come you gots a gun instead of a bow and arrow?" the child said.

"Well," Ben said, smiling, "because my bow and

arrow doesn't fit in this holster I'm wearing. I have to settle for a gun."

"Wow," the boy said. "Do you shoot bad guys?"

"Only if I have to," Ben said. "Are you a bad guy?"

"Me?" the child said, his eyes widening even more. "No. No. I'm good. Honest."

"I'm glad to hear that."

"Jacob," a woman said, hurrying out of the shop, "I told you not to leave the store. Don't ever do that again." She looked up at Ben. "I'm terribly sorry. One minute he was there and the next…"

"He's a real Indian, Mom," Jacob said. "He shoots bad guys with his gun 'cause his bow and arrow doesn't fit in that holster thing."

"Wow," Ben said, chuckling.

The woman smiled. "Thank you for the patience with my son. I do apologize if he said anything to offend you."

"Not at all," Ben said.

"Good," the mother said. "Come on, Jacob."

Ben watched as the pair went on down the sidewalk, the mother still lecturing the inquisitive child about staying close to her.

Cute kid, Ben thought, tugging his Stetson lower on his forehead. He and Laurel had talked about the children they'd have. Two for sure, maybe more. Yeah, they'd daydreamed about a lot of things, all part of the life they would share together. What a joke.

"Aw, hell, forget it," Ben muttered. "It's time to go home."

Ben lived in an A-frame house on two acres of wooded land on the edge of town next to the reservation. The house was set well back from the road, and the entire front of the structure was windows, affording a spectacular view of nature's bounty.

The inside was open and airy with a river-rock fireplace against one wall banked by floor-to-ceiling bookshelves, a half wall dividing the living room from the kitchen, an eating area, small bathroom and laundry room.

The upstairs had a balcony overlooking the downstairs and two large bedrooms with a connecting bath. The second bedroom was an office of sorts, with a computer and more book shelves.

The furniture throughout was big, comfortable and rustic. The gleaming hardwood floors had several large Navajo rugs, and one of Dove Clearwater's woven creations adorned one wall. Scattered among the multitude of books on the shelves were Navajo pots and baskets, all made by people he knew on the rez.

Ben entered the house from the covered garage that led to the kitchen. He went upstairs, changed into jeans and a faded sweatshirt, locked his gun in the metal box on his closet shelf then headed back to the kitchen to find something for dinner.

A short time later he sat at the table and ate a plate-sized omelet filled with ham chunks, green and red peppers, cheese and onions and topped with a generous serving of hot salsa. A tall glass of ice water stood at the ready above the plate.

After eating, he cleaned the kitchen, then settled into his favorite recliner to watch the evening news on television, which failed to hold his attention.

Laurel had never seen this house, he mused, glancing around. What would she think of it? Would she be able to envision herself living here? Or had he decorated with too much of a guy-thing touch to make her feel at ease? Well, that was easy enough to fix. Add some girl-thing doodads, or whatever, to make it evident that a woman was in residence, too.

He'd drawn endless pictures of this dream house while he and Laurel were still in high school, sharing them all with her. They'd decided together which bedroom would be theirs and…

"Damn it, Skeeter," Ben said, smacking the arm of the chair. "Why are you going there? Why are you doing this? And why in the hell are you talking to yourself?"

Ben dragged both hands down his face, then rested his head on the back of the recliner.

Change the mental subject, he ordered himself. Now. *Do not think about Laurel Windsong.* Think about…yes, the robberies at the vacant summer homes.

He'd phoned the sheriffs over in Flagstaff and Prescott on the off chance they were dealing with the same type of crime wave. Both men had said things were quiet on those fronts. It had been a long shot anyway, would have meant that a very sophisticated group was casing an extremely large area of the state to establish which homes were empty during the fall and winter.

No, he thought, this was his problem and whoever was doing it was from Willow Valley or the rez. As much as he hated the truth of that fact, that was the way it was. They were taking things that were easily moved. Televisions, VCRs and DVD players, computers, hunting rifles and ammunition, even microwave ovens.

Why? The stuff wasn't worth much when sold in a dark alley somewhere. It was big risk for small return, which indicated that it was probably kids, teenagers who were bored and out for a thrill that would mess up their futures when he caught them.

And he would catch them, no doubt about it.

He was, Ben knew, bouncing back and forth

between thinking it was one person pulling this off and several who were urging each other on. Whichever was the case, they would make a mistake and he would get them. Oh, yeah, he'd get 'em.

And then tears would flow and hopes for the future would be shattered and lives disrupted for all time.

A sudden image of Laurel appeared in crystal clarity in Ben's mind.

"Yeah, well," he said wearily, "there's a lot of that going around. Decisions are made and pretty puzzles get ruined with no way to put them back together again." He paused. "And, damn it, I'm talking to myself again." He shook his head. "Maybe I should get a dog."

Laurel stomped into the busy kitchen at the Windsong Café and crossed the room to stand next to her mother, who was frying hamburgers and steaks on a large grill.

"One more person," Laurel said, planting her hands on her hips. "If just one more person asks me if I'm going to cut my hair, I'm going to scream the roof down."

Jane smiled as she flipped hamburgers over with the ease of many years of experience.

"You knew it would happen tonight, sweetheart," she said, glancing at Laurel. "I would think you'd have prepared yourself for the fun and games."

"I thought I had, but this is really ridiculous," Laurel said.

"No," Jane said, laughing, "this is Willow Valley. Some things don't change. The love of juicy gossip is one of those. The locals have waited four months for something—anything—to take place between you and Ben, and it finally did. I'm sure he's getting the same nonsense thrown at him as you are."

"He has it coming," Laurel said. "He's the one who opened his big mouth. And I still don't understand why he did it in the first place."

"Don't you?" Jane said, giving her daughter a meaningful look.

"Goodbye," Laurel said, walking away. "I'm not discussing this further. I have customers to keep happy."

"Goodbye," Jane called, laughing again. "Or rather, *hagoonee,* to show off my expertise in speaking Navajo."

May, who was a short, plump woman in her early sixties, took a pie from one of the ovens and set it on a cooling rack.

"Laurel is all in a dither, isn't she?" she said, smiling.

"Yes," Jane said, turning over several steaks on the grill. "Oh, I do wish she and Ben could work out their differences, but ten years is a very long time."

"Not when it comes to love." May laughed. "Jane,

remember when we'd take the babies to the park? We'd spread out a blanket and watch them wiggle and reach for each other. There was Laurel, Ben, Dove and my Joseph. Cute as buttons, every one of them. My goodness, how the years have flown by, haven't they?"

"Yes, they certainly have," Jane said as she served up the hamburgers and steaks.

She carried the plates and red baskets to the pickup ledge in several trips, called for the waitresses waiting for the orders and returned to look at May again.

"Think about it, May," she said. "My Jimmy is gone and so are his parents and mine. Dove's folks were killed in that tragic accident so many years ago. Ben lost his mother and father in that flash flood."

"And Joseph's father flew the coop before Joey was even born." May shook her head. "I'm glad we don't have crystal balls to see into the future or we'd wonder what the point of it all is. Well, Joey is happily married and spoils his two kids rotten, and I'm grateful for that." She paused. "I don't suppose you'll tell me yet why Laurel suddenly came home from Virginia."

"I'm sorry, May," Jane said. "I promised her I wouldn't say a word."

"That's fine. I can wait until she's ready. There's

a sadness in her eyes, though, that breaks my heart, and I don't believe Ben Skeeter has been truly content since Laurel left all those years ago. And Dove? Oh, bless her heart. She had such plans to go to college and study journalism and ended up staying on the rez to raise her twin sisters and her brother. Seventeen years old, she was, and put aside all her dreams to care for those youngsters after their parents were killed."

"Dove has done a fantastic job with her siblings," Jane said, preparing hamburger patties. "Wren is married and has a baby. Robin is studying nursing over in Flagstaff. Eagle is a senior in high school this year. Once he graduates, it will be Dove's turn to live her life the way she wants to. Finally."

"But will she?" May said, pouring corn-bread in-gredients into a large bowl. "Dove is very organized and set in her ways. I suppose she had to be to take care of those kids, but I can't help but wonder if she might just keep on as she is after Eagle graduates. You know, live on the rez in that little house where she grew up, write for the paper now and again, make her rugs and what have you to support herself. I don't believe change will come easy to Dove now."

Jane shook her head. "Oh, wouldn't that be a shame if Dove... Goodness, I don't even want to think about that happening."

"I felt the same way about you after Jimmy died," May said.

"What?" Jane said, looking over at her dear friend.

"I was so hoping that in time you'd marry again, have more babies. But here you are doing exactly the same as when Jimmy was standing next to you. He wouldn't have wanted you to be lonely, Jane, you know that."

"I'm not lonely," Jane said. "I'm very satisfied with my life the way it is." She shook her head. "I just had this conversation with Laurel. What is this? Let's-marry-off-Jane-Nelson-Windsong week?"

May laughed. "Whatever works."

"Oh, hush."

"Just one more thing," May said.

"Hmm?"

"Is Laurel going to cut her hair?"

Late that night Laurel showered, washed the hair that was the topic of conversation then sat on her bed in her pajamas and brushed it in long, steady strokes. She drew her fingers through it as she recalled Ben's words spoken in the café.

Your hair is so beautiful, so silky and…I remember how it felt when I…

She knew exactly what Ben remembered, Laurel thought. After they made love, she'd nestle close to his body and he'd sift his fingers through her hair, watching it fall free, then repeating the motion over and over, never seeming to tire of it.

Sudden heat coursed through Laurel, then pulsed low and hot within her as vivid images of lovemaking shared with Ben taunted her. She moved off the bed and began to pace restlessly around the small room, pulling the brush roughly through her hair.

She couldn't stay in Willow Valley, she thought frantically. She had to leave, put distance between herself and Ben Skeeter. But after what had happened in Virginia, where could she go? What would she do with her life? She adored this pretty little town and the people in it, had always thought she'd live out her days here with Ben and their children. But...

"Oh, God," Laurel said, sinking onto the edge of the bed. "What am I going to do?"

Chapter Three

"I swear, Dove Clearwater," Laurel said, "if I actually catch a fish on the end of this line and that slimy thing comes flying up here, I'm gone. I don't know why I let you talk me into this. I came out here to the rez to have a relaxing Sunday afternoon with you, remember?"

"Fishing *is* relaxing," Dove said. "We're sitting on this nice grass, the water and sky are a lovely shade of blue, the leaves on the tree are gorgeous, it's a crisp fall day. It's your attitude that's not with the program."

"You've got that straight," Laurel said, laughing.

"Well, we could always go back to the house and I'll cut your hair for you."

"Ohhh, don't start with me," Laurel said with a groan. "I'm trying to forget that fiasco with Ben at the café yesterday."

"In my opinion, not that you asked," Dove said, "you two were long overdue to talk to each other like normal people. The stony-silence thing ever since you came back to Willow Valley was ridiculous."

"What happened isn't exactly what I would call a conversation," Laurel said, frowning. "The whole town is buzzing about how Ben Skeeter told Laurel Windsong she shouldn't cut her hair. You cut your hair a few years ago. Did Ben pitch a fit?"

"Nope," Dove said, swinging her head a bit so her shoulder-length dark hair swirled, then settled back into place. "He said it looked very nice. But Ben isn't in love with *me*."

"He's not in love with me, either, Dove," Laurel said quietly. "What we had together was over years ago. What he said in the café about my hair was habit or reflex or whatever. Oh, forget it. I don't want to talk about it anymore."

Laurel paused. "I haven't brought this up because I was waiting to see if you would, but you haven't. So I'll just jump right in. Tell me about your plans."

Laurel looked over at her best friend, seeing a pretty Navajo woman who was about five foot four, small-boned and slender, which made her appear younger than the twenty-seven years old that she was. Her big, dark eyes were her best feature and boasted thick, long lashes.

"What plans?" Dove said, frowning in confusion. "You're right, I haven't mentioned having any plans since you came home."

"Well, surely you're thinking about the future," Laurel said. "The twins are up and gone, and Eagle is a senior in high school. Once he graduates, it will be your turn, Dove. Everything you put on the back burner for the past ten years so you could raise those kids can be brought forward again. You were going to go to college and study journalism, remember?"

Dove shrugged. "That was then."

"What are you saying?" Laurel said, setting her fishing pole next to her on the grass.

"Oh, I don't know, Laurel. I'm not unhappy here on the rez, living in the house I grew up in. I write for the paper when the mood strikes and I'm making a decent living with my weaving. Why rock the boat?"

"There's a big difference between being not unhappy and being happy," Laurel said. "It sounds to me like you're settling for less than what you really want because it's easier to just stay put."

"No, you're wrong," Dove said. "I had such big ideas when I was seventeen, but everything changed when my parents were killed. I raised my brother and the twins, Laurel, and feel like a mother whose last baby bird is going to leave the nest in the spring.

"Yes, it's my turn. My turn to just live a quiet existence without so much responsibility weighing me down. I just don't have the energy left to take on a whole new way of life and head off to college at twenty-seven. I'm doing fine right here."

"Oh, Dove, that paints a picture in my mind of a narrow, lonely existence. You said a couple of weeks ago that you're not even dating anyone."

"Laurel," Dove said, flipping her line in the water to another spot, "think about this. I date someone. I find myself in a relationship at some point and said guy asks me to marry him. We are now looking at hearth, home and babies. Children, Laurel.

"Don't you see? I've raised three kids already. I've done the tooth-fairy bit and helping with homework and pinching pennies to feed us all and putting up with moody teenagers and I don't want to start over with more babies. Any man I might get serious about is going to want a family. I just can't go through all that again."

"But..."

"No."

"You'd feel differently if you were in love," Laurel said.

"No, I wouldn't." Dove paused. "Speaking of plans, do you have any?"

Laurel shook her head. "I'm just doing one day at a time. Dove, I know I'm probably hurting your feelings by not telling you what happened in Virginia to bring me running home, but I just can't talk about it yet."

"I understand that part," Dove said. "I'm here to listen when you're ready to share. I'm just wondering if you intend to just stay on here and work at the café."

"No, and I've told my mother that so she won't be disappointed down the line when I…figure out what to do with my life."

"There are worse things than living in Willow Valley or here on the rez," Dove said. "It's peaceful. Eagle is thinking of joining the Army when he graduates. I think that structured kind of existence would suit him well. He's very restless, edgy, and he wants to leave here as soon as he can. That's fine—for him.

"Me? I'll be more than ready to not have to worry about unpleasant surprises produced by unpredictable teenagers. Each day will go more or less the way I decide it should."

"Dove, that sounds like something an eighty-seven-year-old person would say, not someone who is twenty-seven."

Dove shrugged. "I like the image of it in my mind. I'm going to have control over my own life again. Like I said…peaceful."

"Mmm," Laurel said, frowning.

Several minutes went by in silence, the two friends lost in their own thoughts. The forgotten fishing pole lay unattended on the grass.

"I like Marilyn Montgomery," Laurel said finally. "I met her when I came back and felt an instant bond with her, as though I'd known her for a long time. She said she moved here five years ago, but we never connected during my brief visits from Virginia."

"She's very nice," Dove said, nodding. "And she really spruced up the beauty shop when she bought it. It's popular with locals and tourists."

"She didn't say why she moved to Willow Valley," Laurel said. "And I didn't ask. I figured if she wanted me to know, she'd tell me."

"I don't think anyone knows where she came from or why." Dove laughed. "Not even Cadillac. He called her 'the mystery woman' for a while after she arrived until he got bored with the subject and went on to something else. Anyway, Marilyn is very well liked and respected."

"As well she should be," Laurel said.

"I think I hear someone coming behind that rise," Dove said. "It might be Grandfather. He very often rides his horse on Sunday and he checks to see if I'm fishing in this spot. I want you to know that I put many a Sunday-night meal on the table over the years with the fish I caught here, plus I got to spend time with Grandfather." She cocked her head to one side. "Yes, there is definitely a horse headed our way."

"It's always wonderful to spend time with Grandfather," Laurel said. "Everyone calls him that out of respect. I forget he's really your great-grandfather. Does Eagle realize what an honor it is to be a descendant of a hero, a Navajo code-talker?"

"I don't think Eagle is that impressed by it," Dove said. "Maybe when he's older he'll appreciate what Grandfather and the others did as code-talkers during World War Two. Nothing gets Eagle excited these days except the thought of leaving here." She turned and shaded her eyes with one hand as she looked into the distance. "Yes, that's Thunder, Grandfather's horse. There's no mistaking such a huge black stallion like…but…oops."

"Oops?" Laurel said, turning slightly to look in the same direction that Dove was. "That's—Dove, that's Ben riding Grandfather's horse." She glanced quickly to the left, then the right. "I don't want…"

"Quit looking for a place to hide, for heaven's sake," Dove said with a tsk. "Surely you can greet Ben pleasantly and he'll do the same to you. That's called being mature adults, in case you're wondering."

Laurel glanced at Dove, then looked backward again, realizing that she was sitting in front of a wide tree and, due to the angle that Ben was coming from, there was no way he could see her.

She smoothed her red sweater over the waistband of her jeans, then slid her hands over her head to be certain that no wispy strands had escaped since she'd braided it. She looked over to see Dove giving her a knowing little smile and glared at her again, causing Dove to laugh.

Ben pulled the big horse to a halt about ten feet away, swung off its bare back and dropped the reins to the ground. Thunder immediately began to nibble on the grass.

"Ya at eeh," Ben said, striding toward Dove.

"And greetings to you, too," Dove said, smiling. "Why are you riding Grandfather's horse?"

"I went by to visit with him," Ben said, stopping, "and…" A flash of color caught his eye and he snapped his head around. "Oh. Hello, Laurel. I didn't realize you were here."

"Hello, Ben," she said, then snatched up her pole. "Just doing a little fishing."

"You hate fishing," he said, frowning. "You're afraid you'll catch one and will have to take it off the hook."

"My, my," Dove said, "don't you have a remark-able memory, Benjamin Skeeter."

"Yeah, well." Ben shrugged, removed his Stetson then settled it back on his head. "I'd better be going. I didn't mean to interrupt your conversation."

"Oh, for Pete's sake," Dove said. "You two are being absolutely ridiculous. Ben, sit down and tell us why you're riding Grandfather's horse. Laurel, quit staring at the water like it's the most fascinating thing you've every seen."

"Jeez," Ben said, settling onto the grass. "When you get into your mighty-mother mode, you're like a drill sergeant."

"You'd better believe it, buster," Dove said. "Wren, Robin and Eagle will certainly agree with you on that fact. Now, then…Grandfather? You have his horse?"

Ben frowned. "Yeah. Grandfather said he wasn't feeling well and Thunder needed some exercise. I said I'd take him out and put him through his paces. It has been a long time since I've ridden Thunder and he sure is slowing down. He's getting older, just like the rest of us.

"As for Grandfather, he's just sitting in his favorite chair in his trailer, not doing anything, which isn't like him at all."

"He actually said he wasn't feeling well?" Laurel said, her eyes widening. "Grandfather doesn't complain about anything, ever. Has he seen a doctor?"

"I asked him that," Ben said, "but he ignored me as though I hadn't spoken. He was definitely finished talking, so that was that."

"This is frightening," Dove said, shaking her head. "Everything you're saying is so out of character for Grandfather. I'm going to drive out there and take him some dinner later and see what he'll say to me."

"Good idea." Ben pulled a blade of grass free and nibbled on it for a moment. "He did say one more thing just as I went out the door of his trailer."

"What was it?" Dove said.

Ben tossed aside the blade of grass and sighed.

"Ben?" Laurel said, leaning slightly toward him. "What did Grandfather say?"

"*Neasjah,*" Ben said quietly, meeting Laurel's troubled gaze.

"Owl?" she said. "Grandfather said *owl?*"

"Yeah."

"Oh, dear heaven," Dove said. "Owl means death. I'm going to his trailer right now."

"Dove, wait," Ben said. "I wouldn't do that, because he'll figure out that I saw you and told you he wasn't up to par. He'll clam up, won't say a word. Guaranteed. Stick with your plan to take him some dinner later and see what he'll share with you then."

"Well, all right, I guess," Dove said. "Was he wearing his code-talker medallion like he always does?"

Ben nodded.

"Well, that's one normal thing. But the rest of what you've told us... I saw him last week and he was sitting outside weaving a basket. He seemed fine then."

"I visited him the week before," Laurel said, "and we went for a walk like we usually do, but...now that I look back I realize we didn't go as far as we would on one of our walks. I didn't think anything of it at the time but... Oh, I wish he hadn't said *owl*."

"Let's not panic," Ben said. "We're accustomed to Grandfather being in excellent health. He's in his eighties, you know. It stands to reason that he's slowing down, having some off days, so to speak."

"But why would he say *neasjah?*" Dove said.

"He might not realize he even spoke that aloud," Ben said. "It could be nothing more than the fact that he's spoiled by the great health he's had, too, and is realizing that he's getting up in years, that his next journey will be to the other side."

"No," Dove said, shaking her head.

"Not yet," Laurel said.

"Let's just wait and see what happens," Ben said. "Let's also agree to keep each other posted."

Dove and Laurel frowned and nodded. The trio

was silent for several long moments, each thinking about their beloved Grandfather.

"Oh!" Laurel shrieked suddenly as the fishing pole she was still holding jerked in her hand.

"Hang on tighter," Ben said. "From the way that line is going out and the pole is bending, I'd say you've snagged a good-size one, Laurel."

"I don't want it!" Laurel shrieked, gripping the pole with both hands.

"Don't you dare lose that thing," Dove said. "I definitely want it. I can make Grandfather a super dinner with a freshly caught fish. It's probably a big ole trout, and he loves grilled trout. Start reeling it in, Laurel. Come on."

"I don't know how!" she yelled.

"Ben, help her," Dove said, flopping back on the grass and dissolving in laughter. "This is too funny. Wouldn't you know it would be Laurel who is the champion of the day. Oh, my goodness."

"Pull the pole toward you," Ben said, "at the same time you're reeling in the line."

Laurel leaned back and attempted to turn the handle that would take up the slack of line.

"This isn't working," she said. "The line is going out more, not coming in. That's not a trout, it's a whale."

"Jeez," Ben said, chuckling.

In the next moment he scooted across the grass

and slid behind Laurel, his legs on either side of her as he pressed himself against her, then brought his arms around her to cover her hand on the pole and the other one on the handle.

Dove's eyes widened and sparkled with delight as she saw what Ben had done.

"Oh, my, my," she said. "Thunder is obviously getting nervous from all this shouting." She scrambled to her feet. "I'll go keep him calmed down, walk him out a ways until you two land the whale. Ta-ta."

"Ben, I don't think…" Laurel said.

"Shh," he interrupted. "Concentrate on reeling in Grandfather's dinner. Okay. We're pulling back on the rod at the same time as we're shortening the line. That's it. Slow and easy."

He was a dying man, Ben thought, staring up at the sky for a moment before directing his attention back to what he was doing. Oh, God, Laurel felt good nestled against his body. His body that was going nuts, was on fire with the want, the burning desire for her. Damn, the heat. Low, churning, tightening into a painful coil and…

Mmm, she smelled fantastic with that familiar cologne mixed with fresh air and sunshine. His cheek was resting against her silky hair. Hair that evoked such sensuous memories of when it was freed from the braid, waiting for his hands to sift through it, falling over them both like a waterfall of ebony strands. *Laurel.*

Think fish, Ben told himself. Think about anything except how much he loved this woman and what she was doing to him right now. Fish. Grandfather's dinner.

Ben pulled back on the rod again, then, with his hand still covering Laurel's, reeled in the slackening line that effort had created.

Oh, dear heaven, Laurel thought. She was going to faint dead away. Her heart was racing so fast she could hear the wild tempo echoing in her ears. Her cheeks were flushed pink with warmth, she knew they were. She was encased in the strong embrace of Ben Skeeter and it was wonderful, just exquisite and so very, very wrong or very, very right, she didn't know, couldn't think straight, couldn't...

She wanted him. Oh, how she wanted him. Memories of making love with Ben were slamming against her mind with images so vivid, so real, she could feel his lips on hers, taste him, inhale his special masculine aroma. Her hair was swept free of the braid and caressing them and... Oh, God, the heat that was pulsing so low in her body was... And her breasts ached for Ben's soothing touch, his hands, his mouth, his...

Oh, how she loved Benjamin Skeeter. This was where she belonged. In the arms of her Ben, the man she would marry, who would give her children and a lifetime of happiness they would share. This was how it was meant to be, with all their hopes and dreams coming true one by one as they moved through their days and lovemaking nights together. *Ben*.

Fish. The fish, Laurel thought frantically. The whale. Grandfather's dinner. Focus, Laurel. Focus on the stupid fish.

The fish suddenly flung itself upward out of the water, wiggling in the air before splashing back down again.

"Whoa," Ben said. "Did you see the size of that thing? What a beauty. Grandfather is in for a feast tonight, that's for sure. Pull back...there we go...reel in the line...good, good. We're getting there, Laurel."

Laurel tipped her head to one side and looked up at Ben, realizing too late how close her lips were to his.

"Aren't we...aren't we..." she said, struggling to remember what she wanted to say, "supposed to...have a net...or what...ever?"

"We'll...wing it," Ben said, his voice husky.

Then, before he knew he was going to do it, he lowered his head and captured Laurel's lips in a searing kiss. He parted her lips, his tongue delving into her mouth to be met by hers as she returned the kiss in total abandon. Her lashes drifted down and she savored every sensuous sensation rocketing throughout her heated body. Ben's arousal pressed heavily against her as he deepened the kiss even more.

It was heat. It was ecstasy. It was a kiss they had waited ten years to share and never wished to end. It was memories from the past and a memory being made in the present. And it went on and on.

Ben dropped his hands from Laurel to wrap his arms around her, and she released her hold on the fishing pole to shift enough to encircle his neck with her arms. He lifted his head for a fraction of a second to draw a rough breath, then his mouth melted over Laurel's once again.

The fishing pole slid slowly but surely across the grass and into the water as the fish made its escape. A few moments later the pole was gone and the fish flipped upward again, free of the hook, in a taunting farewell that neither Ben nor Laurel saw. It splashed back into the water and disappeared.

Oh, yes. Yes, Laurel thought hazily. Then reality began to inch into the sexual mist she was encased in. Oh, no. No. What on earth was she doing? She was kissing a man whom she loved with every fiber of her being. A man who hated her with all that he was because he believed she had betrayed him, broken her promises and… No. She mustn't do this. Stop. She had to stop.

Laurel slid her arms from Ben's neck and flattened her hands on his rock-hard chest, pressing enough to cause him to break the kiss and stare at her, desire radiating from the depths of his dark eyes.

"Let me go," she whispered, then drew much-needed air into her lungs. She wiggled in his tight embrace. "Right now. Ben, I mean it."

Ben released her, and she scurried over his leg to sit on the grass several feet away from him, knowing her trembling legs would never support her if she attempted to stand.

Ben took a shuddering breath, tented his legs and rested his head on his knees, striving for control. He lifted his head slowly and looked at Laurel.

"That…that shouldn't have happened," Laurel said, hearing the thread of breathlessness in her voice.

"But it did," Ben said, his voice gritty with passion. "Equally shared. You wanted me as much as I wanted you, and don't even think about trying to deny it."

"We're…we're healthy young people, that's all," Laurel said. "Things got out of hand for a moment there and—it shouldn't have happened, Ben. And it won't happen again. Ten years can't be erased. How we parted back then can't be forgotten. No, this won't happen again."

"We'll see."

"What is that supposed to mean?" she said.

"Forget it," he said, pulling his Stetson low on his forehead. "Just forget the whole damn thing."

"I intend to," she said, deciding to run the risk of getting to her feet. She stood and glanced around. "What happened to the fishing pole?"

Dove peeked around a tree, then came forward, leading Thunder by his reins.

"Hello, hello, I have returned with horse in tow," she said, trying desperately not to giggle. "Where's Grandfather's dinner, mighty fishermen? Or fisher-persons, if you prefer."

Laurel frowned. "I have no idea. The fish ran away, I guess, and took the pole with it. I'll buy you a new pole, Dove. It really was a whale. Big. Very big. And strong. Just booked it out of here and drowned the pole in the process."

"Is that a fact?" Dove said. "My, my, my. Even big, strong Ben Skeeter couldn't hold on to that pole, huh?"

"Nope," Ben said, staring out across the water. "I'll replace the pole, Dove."

"Don't worry about it," Dove said, laughing. "It was an old one of Eagle's that had seen better days."

She became serious and tapped one fingertip against her chin. "However, I do believe that there is something of much greater importance to discuss than a rickety old fishing pole."

"No, there isn't," Ben and Laurel said in unison.

"No?" Dove said, raising her eyebrows. "Then answer this question, dear friends." She looked pointedly at Laurel, then Ben, both of whom averted their eyes from hers. Dove burst into laughter again. "What am I going to fix Grandfather for dinner?"

"That's it," Ben said, rolling to his feet. "I'm gone. Out of here. See ya."

He took Thunder's reins from Dove, swung up onto the horse's bare back, pulled on the reins to turn Thunder then clicked his tongue at the horse and took off at a gallop.

Laurel folded her arms beneath her breasts, tapped one foot, stared at the sky, the grass, then finally looked at Dove.

"All I have to say is," Laurel said, lifting her chin, "I suggest you make Grandfather a dinner of corn bread and soup. Now, if you'll excuse me, Dove, I do believe I'll go home. Goodbye. I'll see you soon."

"Ta-ta," Dove said, wagging the fingers of one hand. "Thank you for a most interesting afternoon, Laurel."

Laurel marched past her with her nose in the air. Dove turned and watched her until she disappeared from view, then punched one fist in the air before dancing a little jig.

"Yes," she said. "Yes, yes, yes. They're goners, both of them. Now all they have to do is realize they're still madly in love with each other. Yes, yes, yes."

Chapter Four

At eight o'clock that evening Jane Windsong pressed a button on the remote and turned off the television that she and Laurel were watching.

"All right, young lady," Jane said. She shifted on her end of the sofa to look at her daughter, who was curled up on the other end. "That was deep sigh number ten or twelve or whatever. Add that performance to the three words, maximum, you spoke during dinner and it doesn't take a genius to figure out there's something troubling you. Didn't you enjoy your afternoon with Dove?"

"Sure I did," Laurel said, picking an imaginary

thread off her jeans. "Dove and I always have fun together. I caught a giant fish. Sort of. I mean, it snarfed up the cheese on my hook and flopped around in the water for a while, but it got away. There you go." She sighed again. "The one who got away."

"And just when did Ben show up where you and Dove were fishing?" Jane said.

"He came on Grandfather's horse because—" Laurel looked over at her mother. "I didn't say anything about Ben being there."

"The one *who* got away?" Jane said, raising her eyebrows. "Since when is a fish a *who* instead of a *that?*"

"Well, thank you, Detective Windsong," Laurel said, frowning. "You've been reading too many of those mystery novels you like so much."

"I was right, wasn't I? So. Ben popped onto the scene at the lake and then what? Did you actually manage to carry on a civil conversation?"

"Among other things," Laurel mumbled.

"I heard that."

"No, you didn't." Laurel pulled her braid forward, removed the elastic from the end and began to unwind the thick strands. "Anyway, the civil conversation part was centered on Grandfather. Ben was riding Thunder—who is definitely showing his age—because Grandfather said he wasn't feeling well and his horse needed the exercise."

"Grandfather actually said he wasn't feeling well?" Jane said, frowning.

"Yes, and Ben heard him say *neasjah,* although Ben isn't certain that Grandfather is aware he said it aloud. Ben, Dove and I are really worried about Grandfather. Dove is taking dinner to him this evening to see how he is. He *was* wearing his code-talker medallion, which is good."

"Oh, honey," Jane said, "he's worn that award since the day he received it. It would be like part of getting dressed by now. I don't think too much emphasis should be placed on his wearing the medallion. I'm definitely going to go out to the rez to see him this coming week. He's not a young man anymore, Laurel. We all have to realize that."

"I don't want to," Laurel said, tugging harder on her hair.

Jane laughed. "Don't you sound like a bratty three-year-old. Come to think of it, you were a rather bratty kid when you were three."

"Oh, thanks a lot," Laurel said, smiling.

"What's this? A smile? Call the newspaper with this bulletin."

"Mother, cut it out," Laurel said, laughing. "I'm sorry if I've been grumpy since I got back from being with Dove. Okay? I just have a lot on my mind. You know, I'm worried about Grandfather and…and…Ben and I… See, the fish was really big and I didn't know how to…so Ben sat behind me to help me reel in the dumb thing…but then I turned my head to ask him something and… I really don't want to talk about this."

"Mmm," Jane said, squinting at the ceiling for a long moment before looking at Laurel again. "All the clues indicate that Ben Skeeter kissed you. No, to be more precise, you and Ben *shared* a kiss. You said 'Ben and I' before."

"The FBI needs you, Mother," Laurel said, glaring at Jane. "I wish you'd stop doing that *CSI* number of yours. It's very annoying."

"So noted. But now that the facts are on the table… You and Ben kissed and…?"

"And it shouldn't have happened, that's what," Laurel said, getting to her feet and beginning to pace around the small living room. "It was a mistake and I'm erasing it from my mind."

"Why was it a mistake?"

Laurel stopped in her tracks and looked at her mother.

"Because I'm still in love with him," Laurel said, nearly shouting. "And he hates me so—" She smacked one hand on her forehead. "I can't believe

I just said that. I do not believe that I opened my big mouth and announced that I'm—"

"Still in love with Ben Skeeter?" Jane said. "Good grief, Laurel, I'd have to be stupid not to already know that."

"You would?"

"Oh, Laurel, for heaven's sake. If you didn't love Ben, you wouldn't have been breaking your neck to stay out of his way for the past four months. And the same goes for him, too. If he didn't care, he would have started a conversation with you the first time he saw you after you came home.

"Why do you think everyone has been watching you and Ben so closely? They're all waiting for you two to admit the old feelings are still alive and well, then act accordingly, which apparently happened at the lake today."

"No, you're wrong," Laurel said. "Everyone is wrong. Ben hates the very air that I breathe because I left here ten years ago. Left him."

"Then why did he kiss you?" Jane said.

"Because I was an inch away at the time. It was a reflex kind of a thing that—I repeat—should not have happened. And won't happen again. Never." Laurel sighed a very sad-sounding sigh. "Ever."

"Oh," Jane said, dipping her head to hide her smile.

"Maybe I'll go to bed," Laurel said, slouching

back onto the sofa. "No, that's silly. I'm not tired. Why don't you turn the television back on?"

"I want to discuss something with you first," Jane said.

"Okay. What?"

"Well, I know you didn't want to attempt to drive across country in your clunker car when you came home so you sold it in Virginia. You also sold all your furniture because you didn't want any reminders of your time spent there."

"That's right."

"The thing is, Laurel, it's not working out for you to continually borrow my car. You had it all afternoon on the rez, and I realized I needed to go to the grocery store but had no way to get there. I think you should buy yourself a vehicle."

Laurel sat up straight on the sofa. "But I wouldn't know what to get because I don't know where I'm going to live or what I'll be doing. Do I want a vehicle that can handle the snow here or just a little compact car to zip around a city in? I can't make that decision yet."

"Honey," Jane said gently, "that's my point. You're refusing to make decisions about anything of consequence, and that's not good, not moving forward with your life one iota. So I'm going to push you into making a choice about a vehicle. You have to start somewhere, Laurel."

"No, I'm not ready." Laurel paused. "You're right. I have to start somewhere. Would you like to go over to Flagstaff with me tomorrow and look at cars? You didn't schedule either of us to work at the café."

"No, I don't think that's a good idea," Jane said. "Neither one of us knows a thing about vehicles. There's more to buying one than kicking the tires. When I bought the car I'm driving now, Ben went with me. He knew all the questions to ask and what to watch for during a test drive. I've been very pleased with the one I've got."

"Oh, no way," Laurel said, crossing her arms over her breasts. "Like I'm really going to ask Ben Skeeter to help me pick out a car. Not in this lifetime, Mother."

Jane shrugged. "He's the best man for the job. Of course, he may have to work. Or there's the possibility that he wouldn't want to spend that much time with you since you're so convinced he hates you with a passion."

"He wouldn't have to speak to me," Laurel said. "No, forget it. It's a ridiculous idea." She paused. "Then again, it would be strictly business. No. No way. But I am a mature woman who is perfectly capable of setting aside my personal feelings for Ben and concentrating on the purpose for the outing. I would expect the same from him."

"I see," Jane said, smothering a bubble of laughter. "That's very mature of you, dear. Of course, the news will spread like wildfire if you two go off for the day."

"I've had enough of worrying about what people are thinking about me and Ben," Laurel said. "Let them go nuts. They will, of course, because look what a dither everyone got in after the don't-cut-your-hair fiasco.

"If I'm going to start taking steps to move forward with my life I can't allow myself to be dictated to by a town full of bored people who thrive on gossip. So there."

"That's fine, very good. Then you'll ask Ben to help you select a vehicle? That's a wise choice and I'm glad you made it."

"Me, too. I'll go call him right now." Laurel got to her feet. "I don't know his phone number."

"It's in the book. You haven't seen the house Ben had built. We had a housewarming for him and it's absolutely gorgeous. You can't see it from the road, so maybe he'll invite you to take a tour."

"No, he won't, and I have no desire to see it, anyway," Laurel said. "He always wanted an A-frame home with lots of windows and a loft type of thing. Is that what he... Never mind. I don't really care. I'm focused on getting a vehicle and that's it. I'm asking the most knowledgeable person in that arena to assist me. It's very simple."

As Laurel headed for the kitchen to find the telephone book and make the call, Jane smiled and patted herself on the shoulder.

"Jane Nelson Windsong," she said, "you're good. That was brilliant. Ah, yes, it's nice to know that I haven't lost my touch."

Ben sat in his favorite chair and scraped the last bite of ice cream from the big bowl he was holding as he watched an old made-for-television movie.

He and Laurel had watched this movie together years ago when it had first been released, he mused. He remembered how she'd curled up next to him on the sofa in her living room as they'd shared a batch of popcorn. Jane hadn't been home that evening, although he couldn't recall where she had gone.

Yeah, he'd seen this movie with Laurel and he knew how it ended. What he hadn't known at the time was how his relationship with Laurel Windsong was going to end. The people in the movie were destined to live happily ever after. Ben Skeeter? Hell.

The telephone rang, bringing him from his gloomy thoughts. In the next instant he frowned, hoping it wasn't one of his deputies needing him to come assist in a problem situation. He strode into the kitchen and snatched up the receiver to the telephone that was sitting on the end of the counter.

"Sheriff Skeeter," he said, setting down the bowl and spoon.

"Ben? Hello, this is..."

"Laurel," Ben said, then grimaced in self-disgust as he realized he'd just revealed that he still recognized her voice on the phone. "Isn't it?"

"Yes. Yes, it is. I...um...I have a favor to ask of you, Ben. It's a business proposition, really. I need the best advice I can get in regard to purchasing a vehicle, and you are an expert about such things. If you'd be willing to go to Flagstaff to help me, I'll pay for your gas and lunch. I'm continually inconveniencing my mother by borrowing her car. Well?"

"I see," Ben said, hooking his free hand on the back of his neck. "You do realize that people will talk if we go off together for the day."

"I'm tired of worrying about what people are saying or not saying. I need a car. You're the best person to help me select one. And that is that. Strictly business. As long as you and I know that, the heck with the gossips."

This was stupid, Ben thought. A whole day alone with Laurel? A whole day of not being able to kiss her again, not touch her, not pull her into his arms and...really dumb.

But then again, maybe not. During those hours he'd be beaten over the head with her lack of caring for him. Strictly business, she'd said. That just might help get the message through to his mind—and his heart—that Laurel Windsong didn't care about him, hadn't in over ten years. Yeah, this just might be a good idea.

"Ben?"

"Okay, Laurel. I'll help you select a vehicle. I'm off tomorrow."

"You are? Oh, well, so am I. What time is convenient for you?."

"I'll pick you up at nine tomorrow morning."

"Fine. Thank you, Ben. Oh, one other thing. I haven't called Dove yet to ask what happened when she took dinner to Grandfather. Have you spoken to her?"

"Yes, I called her. She said that Grandfather thanked her for the meal but didn't really seem to want to chat, so she left."

"But he loves to have company."

"Not tonight."

"I'm really worried about him, Ben."

"Well, the three of us are going to have an eye on him and keep each other posted so we can hopefully figure out what is going on with Grandfather. He may be fine in a few days."

"I hope so," Laurel said. "I'll let you go. Thank you for being willing to help me tomorrow. I really do appreciate it."

"Yeah. Good night, Laurel."

"Good night, Ben."

Ben replaced the receiver very slowly, then didn't release his hold on it, not wanting to totally break the connection with Laurel.

Aw, damn, he thought, finally snatching his hand away. He loved her so much. He couldn't go on like this, because it was ripping him to shreds and had been ever since she'd come home. Tomorrow had to help him, it just had to. All those hours would be spent with Laurel treating him like anyone else she'd grown up with. Nothing more, nothing less. Just a guy.

A guy she'd kissed the socks off of by the lake today.

No, he wasn't going there. He'd like to believe that kiss meant something, but it really didn't. It had caught them both off guard, just happened, and they'd responded. Man, had they responded. But Laurel had been very quick to make it clear that it was a mistake and wouldn't happen again. So, okay, he didn't have to get hit with a brick to get the message.

And tomorrow they'd go to Flagstaff and he'd be forced to endure hours of Laurel treating him like…just a guy.

* * *

The next morning brought a chilling wind that pushed puffs of ominously dark clouds across a gray sky. Multitudes of colorful leaves were whipped off the trees, then flung everywhere.

After what had proven to be a restless night's sleep, Laurel dressed in jeans, a cable-knit pink sweater and tennis shoes. She brushed her hair until it shone, then created her usual single braid that hung down her back. She set her purse and a navy-blue windbreaker on the sofa, then headed for the kitchen for a cup of coffee.

"Good morning, honey," Jane said, glancing up from the newspaper she was reading at the table. "It's not a very nice day for your outing. A cold front must have snuck in during the night, because there wasn't anything about this change in weather on the news."

"It doesn't matter," Laurel said, sitting opposite her mother with a mug of coffee. "I don't need sunshine to pick out a car. I've decided to get something that can handle icy roads. Even if I move to Phoenix or somewhere warm like that, I'll still want to be able to visit you without having to worry about the driving conditions."

"That's good thinking," Jane said, setting the newspaper aside. "I must say, though, I can't picture you living in Phoenix. You've always enjoyed the changing seasons so much here in Willow Valley." She laughed. "I still remember the time that you, Dove and Ben were about six, I think, and spent the day with Grandfather so you could build him a huge snowman."

"Ah, yes," Laurel said, smiling at the memory. "It was a huge snowman, all right, and we were so proud of that creation."

"Until..." Jane laughed again and shook her head.

"Until the dumb thing fell over and buried the three of us in cold, wet snow." Laurel sighed. "We were such happy children, without a care in the world. We were all cherished and cared for, protected and nurtured by parents who loved us beyond measure. But then we grew up and fell prey to the coyote."

"The coyote?" Jane said, raising her eyebrows. "You're indulging in Navajo beliefs this morning?"

"Yes, I guess I am. The coyote is a trickster, crafty and clever, and is not to be trusted. Nothing turned out the way the three of us planned because of the coyote."

"Also known as life, my sweet," Jane said, smiling gently.

"I know."

"Are you still comfortable with the idea of this outing with Ben today, Laurel?"

"Somewhere in the middle of the night I decided it was a very good idea to spend the day with Ben," Laurel said. "I've been avoiding him like a frightened child ever since I came home. It's time for me to start acting like a mature woman, for heaven's sake.

"I'm still in love with Ben. He is definitely not in love with me, and I need to accept that, deal with it and move on. These hours today with Ben will emphasize that what we once shared is over, was finished years ago. This trip to Flagstaff is good therapy for me."

"Spoken like a true psychologist," Jane said.

"No, spoken like a woman who is still nursing wounds that should have healed a long time ago. I'm taking control of my life, including my emotions, as we speak."

"I see," Jane said. "Well, keep one eye open for the coyote as you turn over that new leaf."

"I intend to."

The doorbell rang and Laurel jerked in her chair at the sudden noise.

"That's Ben," Laurel said, her eyes widening.

"I imagine it is," Jane said, nodding.

"Right on time," Laurel said, glancing at the clock on the wall. "Ben has always been very punctual."

"Yes, he has." Jane paused. "Don't you think you should go open the front door?"

"Oh," Laurel said, jumping to her feet. "Yes. Of course. I'm going to do that. Right now."

Jane laughed softly as Laurel left the kitchen.

* * *

At the door Laurel hesitated, drew a steadying breath, then produced what she hoped was a pleasant smile. She opened the door and the smile vanished.

Oh, mercy, she thought, look at him. Ben Skeeter in jeans, a black sweater, Stetson tugged low on his forehead and an unbuttoned fleece-lined suede jacket, was a sight to behold. He was just so incredibly...male.

"Good morning, Laurel," Ben said quietly, looking directly into her eyes. "Ready to go?"

With you? Laurel thought foggily. Anywhere.

"Laurel?"

"Huh? Oh. Yes, I'm all set. Come in. I just have to get my jacket and purse. I was going to take a windbreaker, but from what you're wearing, I'm guessing it's colder out there than I thought."

"It's pretty nippy," Ben said as he entered the house.

"I'll get a heavier jacket," Laurel said, closing the door as Jane came into the living room.

"Hello, Ben," Jane said as Laurel went to collect another coat.

"Jane," he said, touching the fingertips of one hand to the brim of his Stetson.

"I was thinking of visiting Grandfather today," Jane said. "Laurel said he hasn't been feeling well."

"He's not up to par, that's for sure," Ben said. "He may not want company, but it's worth a try."

Jane nodded.

"Okay, we're off," Laurel said, returning wearing a puffy red jacket. "Bye, Mom."

"Enjoy your day," Jane said.

As the door closed behind Laurel and Ben, Jane stared at it for a long moment.

"Together," she whispered, "they're stronger than the coyote."

Ben's vehicle was a black Chevy Tahoe that he'd equipped with a police radio beneath the dashboard. He also had a portable blue light that he could put on the roof if he wasn't driving a patrol car while on duty.

"This is a big machine," Laurel said, glancing around as Ben drove away from the house. "I don't want anything this enormous. I would like something that handles well in snow, though."

Ben nodded. "SUVs, vans and trucks with four-wheel drive come in all sizes." He paused. "You…um…plan to live where there's snow?" Like right here in Willow Valley?

"I don't know," Laurel said, looking out the side window. "But I do want to be able to visit my mother no matter what the weather is."

"Oh. Yeah, that makes sense." Ben paused.

"Why don't you have a car now? Didn't you need one in Virginia?"

"I sold it before I came home," Laurel said, switching her gaze to the front window, "along with my furniture and what have you. I shipped my clothes, got on a plane and here I am."

"Why?"

"Why what?" Laurel said, still not looking at Ben.

"Why did you sell everything? And why did you come home?"

"It was time for a change," she said quietly.

"So you quit your job without having another one lined up?"

"Yes, Ben, I did," she said, an edge to her voice as she finally looked at him. "End of story. I don't intend to spend the day being interrogated."

"I'm chatting, not interrogating," he said, frowning.

"Fine. Chat about something else."

"Whew. You're a tad touchy on the subject of Laurel Windsong, aren't you?"

"I just don't wish to discuss my personal business, that's all. So. Let's talk about you. You achieved your dream, your goal, of being a police officer. Is it everything you hoped it would be? Is it difficult to be in charge of both Willow Valley and the rez? Did you have an A-frame house built, like you always intended to? Why haven't you married and started a family?"

"Whoa, there, Miss Marple," Ben said, chuckling. "And you accuse *me* of interrogating *you?*"

"I'm just chatting."

"Okay, I get it. Tit for tat. The difference between us is I don't have any secrets and you obviously do. So, yes, being sheriff is everything I'd hoped it would be. Yes, having responsibility for both Willow Valley and the rez is a big load, but I have very good deputies on the payroll. Yes, my house is an A-frame, just like the pictures I used to draw and show you. There."

"You didn't answer the last question," Laurel said, looking at him intently. "About why you haven't married and started a family."

Ben pressed harder on the gas pedal as he eased into the traffic on the interstate highway.

Because, Laurel, he thought, his jaw tightening, *I'm still in love with you and can't imagine sharing a life with anyone else. And unless I can move past that somehow, I'm facing a lot of lonely years, just like the last ten years have been.*

He shrugged. "I just haven't had time to devote to thinking about a wife and kids. But I will. Someday. My job keeps me very busy. And you? Weren't there any eligible men in Virginia?"

"My job kept me very busy," Laurel said, looking out the side window again.

And none of the men I met were you, Ben, she thought.

Neither spoke for the next fifteen minutes.

"Red," Laurel said finally, causing Ben to jerk slightly at the sudden sound of her voice.

"What?" he said, glancing over at her, then back at the traffic.

"I want a red car. Yes, definitely a red one."

"Oh, boy," Ben said, smiling. "So that means if we find a really great deal on a good vehicle, you'll pass if it isn't red?"

"Yep."

"Dandy," he said, shaking his head. "Do you want new, or used?"

"A new one, so that it's covered under all the warranties."

"That's smart," he said, nodding.

"I'm a very intelligent woman."

"Yeah, I know you are, Laurel," Ben said seriously. "A person doesn't get to be a psychologist by taking a bunch of easy courses. I respect that."

"Thank you."

"Laurel, I'd like the answer to one question that comes under the heading of your personal business. Just one. I never asked you this and...okay? One question?"

"It depends on what it is," she said, frowning at him.

"My question is, why did you decide to go to college so far away from—" *Me*. "—from Willow Valley? You could have gone to Flagstaff, Tucson or Phoenix. Why did you go all the way to Virginia?"

"I didn't have any choice in the matter. I told you that at the time."

"No, you didn't."

"Yes, I'm sure I did, Ben. What difference does it make? You were furious that I was leaving at all, so why bring it up now?"

"No, I was blown away by the fact that you were putting the entire country between us. If you were so determined to get your degree and had chosen a school closer to home, we could have compromised, worked something out and— What do you mean you didn't have any choice in the matter?"

"You're twisting the facts," Laurel said, her voice rising. "You said that if I left Willow Valley we were through, finished."

"No, I said if you went to Virginia—which would mean you couldn't come home every weekend—we were finished. Big difference there, Ms. Windsong."

"That's not what you said, Mr. Skeeter."

"Yes, it was, damn it, and you chose Virginia anyway."

"I didn't want to go that far away," Laurel said, nearly shouting. "But Mr. Chapman, our high school principal, found out there was grant money in Virginia for female minorities with top grades.

"I'm half Navajo and had straight A's. I went to Virginia because I got a scholarship to go there and it meant I didn't have to work as well as attend college, which would have made it impossible to get my degree in the usual amount of time.

"Do you get it now, Ben? Do you see why I didn't have any choice in the matter? I went after my dream, just as you did, and I wanted to accomplish that goal as quickly as possible so I could…could come home again." *To you.* "But you ended our relationship because I was leaving. I told you why it had to be Virginia."

"I…" Ben cleared his throat while aware of the increased tempo of his now racing heart. "I didn't hear you say those words, Laurel. I guess nothing registered beyond that fact that you were going away, not following the plan we'd made for our future together. Going as far away as you possibly could."

"No, Ben," she said quietly, "it wasn't like that. Dear heaven, all these years you thought that I— You would have been willing to compromise if I'd gone to school in Flagstaff or Phoenix? You didn't tell me that."

"Why bother? You'd already said you were going to Virginia," he said, his grip on the steering wheel tightening to the point that his knuckles turned white. "I don't believe this. We lost everything we had together, our hopes and plans, our future, because of a misunderstanding, a lack of proper communication?"

"I guess so," Laurel said, her voice trembling as she felt the color drain from her face. "Dear God, Ben, what have we done?"

"Shattered dreams," he said, his voice hoarse as a pulse ticked wildly in his temple. "Dreams that can never be put back together again."

Because you no longer love me. But I still love you, Laurel thought, turning her head to hide the tears shimmering in her eyes. *Oh, Ben.*

Dreams that can never be put back together again because, Ben thought, an achy sensation seizing his throat, *while I didn't stop loving you, you're no longer in love with me. And that, as the saying goes, is that. Aw, damn it, Laurel.*

Chapter Five

The drive from Willow Valley to Flagstaff took approximately ninety minutes if the traffic was light and the weather didn't require a slower, safer speed.

The remaining half hour left in the journey after Ben and Laurel's incredible revelations about what had happened ten years before was made in total and oppressive silence. They were each lost in their own thoughts, replaying what they had just learned and attempting to deal with it.

She would not, Laurel decided as the skyline of Flagstaff came into view, dwell on this any longer. She would not indulge in useless if-only scenarios.

The outcome was still the same, the damage had been done and couldn't be repaired. They had, just as Ben said, shattered their dreams, and they couldn't be put back together again.

Ben merged into the busy traffic in the city and went several blocks before parking on a side street next to a car dealership. He turned off the ignition and folded his arms on top of the steering wheel.

"I've been trying to accept what we've discovered today," he said, looking over at Laurel, "the way I believe Grandfather would, because I respect him so much. I think he would say that what happened was what was meant to be. I can't be positive, of course, that that would be his conclusion, but I'm going with it."

"I see," Laurel said quietly. "Well, that's good. I hope we can...we can at least...be friends, Ben, instead of spending so much time and energy trying to keep out of each other's way."

"Friends," Ben said, gazing up at the gray sky for a long moment. "Right."

"Right," Laurel said miserably.

"Maybe," he said, opening the door. "Let's go see if we can find you a spiffy red vehicle."

No, Laurel thought, getting out and closing the door, let's go home so she could crawl into bed and not emerge for five years or so. Friends. How was she supposed to behave like a buddy around the man who possessed her heart? How was she supposed to do that? Oh, this was going to be a horrendous day. She could only hope that a red car was sitting on this lot about to call her name.

But it was three dealerships and three hours later before Laurel finally found the car she wanted. It was a bright red Dodge Caravan minivan, which was the smaller model of the vans offered. She and Ben took it for a test drive, with both of them taking a turn behind the wheel.

"Handles well," Ben said, nodding as he pulled back onto the lot. "It doesn't have as much storage room and bells and whistles as the bigger model, but I think it will serve your purposes and should be okay on winter roads. What do you think?"

"It smells good," Laurel said. "Don't you love the smell of new vehicles?"

Ben chuckled. "Well, that settles it, then. It passed the smell-good test and it's red. Hey, what more could you want?"

"I'm going to buy it," she said, nodding decisively. "Yes. It feels good to be making a major decision, too. I've just been floating along in a limbo state ever since I came back to Willow Valley. My mother knew what she was doing when she insisted that it was time I bought my own transportation."

Ben nodded, then turned off the ignition, which

was the signal for the salesman to hustle over to where they had parked on the lot.

"Well, folks?" the man said, smiling as Ben and Laurel got out of the van. "What's the verdict?"

"I'll take it," Laurel said. "I'll make a down payment and finance the rest."

"You've made a wise choice," the salesman said. "I think you'll be very happy with this vehicle. Let's go into my office and get the paperwork tended to, shall we?"

The documents were signed, then the salesman said he wanted to have the van washed before Laurel drove it off the lot.

"No problem," Ben said. "We're ready for lunch. We'll be back in an hour."

"That'll do it," the salesman said, shaking Laurel's hand. "We'll get your new baby all shined up, Ms. Windsong. It got a bit dusty on the lot, then it rained and, well, it will be sparkling by the time you return."

"Thank you," Laurel said.

She and Ben left the dealership and a short time later were sitting in a booth and placing orders for lunch in a Mexican restaurant. Laurel dipped a corn tortilla chip in a small bowl of salsa and popped it into her mouth.

"Mmm," she said. "Just as good as I remember. This is my favorite restaurant in Flagstaff."

"Mine, too," Ben said.

"I know," Laurel said, reaching for another chip.

"You know a great deal about me," Ben said quietly. "I remember when I told you everything that was on my mind, big, little and in between."

"That was a long time ago, Ben," Laurel said, fiddling with her spoon. "There's no purpose to be served by talking about the past. What's done is done. We'd both do well to adopt what you believe would be Grandfather's philosophy about what happened. We just weren't meant to be together, to have what we were so sure back then was right for us." She paused. "I don't think we should discuss this again."

"Yeah," Ben said, turning to look out the window of the restaurant. "Okay."

"Are...are we going to at least be friends, Ben?"

"I don't know, Laurel," he said, meeting her gaze. "I really don't know the answer to that right now."

"Plates are hot, folks," the waitress said, appearing at the table. "There you go. Enjoy your lunch."

Laurel picked up her fork and stared at the cheese enchiladas she'd ordered, realizing her appetite had vanished. She forced herself to take a bite, produced a smile of approval and shoveled in another forkful.

Ben ate half of his selection of a bean burrito and three beef tacos, then pushed his plate to one side. He sank back in the booth and folded his arms over his chest.

"What's wrong, Ben?" Laurel said. "I've never seen you leave even one tiny morsel on your plate when we've eaten here."

"What's wrong? I'm not hungry." He leaned forward and crossed his arms on the table. "What's wrong? I'm not Grandfather. I'm not as wise and full of wisdom as he is. I'm just plain old Benjamin Skeeter, who is mad as hell about what happened ten years ago, Laurel. We thought we were so connected, like...like one entity, soul mates, and it turns out we didn't even know how to talk, communicate with each other. Soul mates? What a joke."

"We were so young then, Ben," Laurel said, a frantic edge to her voice. "We made a mistake. We listened, but we didn't really hear what the other one was saying because we were focused on our own agendas. It's very sad, but being angry isn't going to change anything. Maybe we would have been miserable together if we'd gotten married."

"Do you honestly believe that?" he said, leaning closer to her.

"I...I don't know. I just don't know. We'll never know, Ben, because we're not the same people now that we were then. Ten years is a long time, and we've changed, both of us. We're almost like strangers, really. Yes, we have a history, but we don't have a present or...or a future together."

"Strangers," Ben said, a rough edge to his voice. "Just what do you suggest we do with all the memories that belong to the history part you're referring to, Laurel? How do we forget what it was like to make love together? Answer me that."

"Ben, don't," Laurel whispered. "Please. Just don't."

"I can't sit here anymore," Ben said, sliding out of the booth. "Finish your lunch and I'll meet you back at the car lot."

"No, Ben, wait," Laurel said. "I can't eat this. I'm paying for lunch, like I promised."

Ben snatched up the check from the table. "Like you promised? Promised? I don't think you know the definition of that word, Laurel."

Laurel got to her feet. "Don't you dare say that. What happened was as much your fault as it was mine." She glanced quickly around and saw that several customers were staring at them. "Let's get out of here."

Ben tossed some bills on the table for a tip, then strode to the register at the entrance of the restaurant and paid the check. Laurel followed him, her heart aching as she struggled against threatening tears. They made the three-block walk back to the car dealership in total silence. Before entering the lot, Ben stopped and Laurel halted next to him, looking up at him questioningly.

"I need time to deal with what came to light today," he said, his voice flat. "Right now I'm just mad as hell, and that's not a good place to be. Just…just stay out of my way until I can get a grip on this."

"But…"

"Keep away from me, Laurel," he said, tugging his Stetson low on his forehead. "Do you understand? Just keep the hell away from me."

Ben started off again, heading for the office on the car lot. Laurel hardly remembered the enthusiastic chatter of the salesman, who handed her a folder with her copies of the paperwork, then gave her the keys to the van as he beamed. She thanked him, he thanked her, then Ben told her to follow him back to Willow Valley on the off chance she had problems driving a vehicle she wasn't familiar with yet.

"Yes, all right," Laurel said, not really looking at Ben. "I appreciate your coming with me today and making certain I get home safely."

"I'd do the same for any stranger," Ben said, then turned and strode to where he'd parked his Tahoe.

As they drove out of Flagstaff, a funny little bubble of laughter escaped from Laurel's lips as she realized that the jacket she was wearing was the exact same shade as her new van.

"Is that cute or corny?" she said, then sniffled.

Laurel Windsong, she thought, don't you dare start crying. She'd drive her super-duper new van right into a tree if she started blubbering like an idiot.

But she was just so sad.

To think that Ben would have been willing to compromise about her wanting a degree in psychology if she'd gone to a college closer to Willow Valley, but believed she'd chosen to put as much distance between them as possible on purpose was just so incredibly sad.

She'd told him about the scholarship to Virginia, but he hadn't heard her say the words, had stopped comprehending what she'd been saying when he'd realized she was leaving.

God, ten years. Ten years of heartache, of sleepless nights and hours of weeping, all because of a misunderstanding. Ben was right, she thought miserably, it was a lot to deal with, so difficult to find a place to put the truth of what had really happened.

She'd gotten stuck on the emotion of sorrow. Ben was engulfed in anger to the point that he'd ordered her to stay away from him. Shattered dreams. Ten years. And now they were strangers. She was in love with the Ben of then but didn't really know the Ben of now. And that was very, very sad.

* * *

When Laurel and Ben were about twenty minutes outside of Willow Valley, he put on his turn signal and left the interstate on the off-ramp to a rest stop. He lowered the window on the Tahoe and motioned for Laurel to follow him.

Laurel frowned, wondering if he could see something wrong with the van that she wasn't aware of. She parked next to Ben and got out of the van, meeting him at the rear of her vehicle.

"What's wrong?" she said. "Am I getting a flat tire or something?"

"No, no, the van is fine," he said, "and you're handling it very well."

Ben took off his Stetson, raked one hand through his hair and settled the Stetson back into place. A chill wind whipped across the parking lot, and Laurel shivered.

"Then why did we stop?" she said, wrapping her hands around her elbows. "I'm freezing."

Ben sighed and stared up at the dark clouds for a long moment before meeting Laurel's confused gaze.

"I...I was pretty rough on you back there in Flagstaff," he said, sounding weary. "I've been going over and over it since we started home and I want to apologize for ripping into you like that." He shook his head. "You were right, Laurel. What happened was as much my fault as it was yours. I dumped all the blame on you, and that wasn't fair."

"Well," Laurel said, her voice quivering slightly, "thank you for that, Ben."

"But one thing remains true," he continued. "We *are* strangers. Yeah, we have memories of things—of sharing— What I'm trying to say here is that those memories belong to people who existed ten years ago. We're not those people anymore."

"No, we're not."

"Forget what I said about keeping away from me," he said, frowning. "That was raw emotions talking and it was uncalled for. We'll see each other around town, be polite, compare notes with Dove about what we find out about Grandfather's health, be civil, for heaven's sake."

"Just as strangers who have just met would be," Laurel said, looking down at the tips of her tennis shoes. "Is that what you're saying, Ben?"

"Yeah. I guess that about sums it up."

"Sure," Laurel said, drawing a line in the dirt with the toe of one shoe. "That makes sense. Strangers being polite and… Fine. That's clear enough."

"Okay." Ben nodded. "Listen, I was wondering if I could stop by your house on the way into town and find out what your mother thinks after visiting

Grandfather today. Maybe she'll have a good report, tell us that he was glad to see her, invited her in for a chat. You know, behaving as he normally would. Would you mind if I came by before I go home?"

"No, not at all," Laurel said, looking up at him. "I'll see you at the house."

"Do you realize that your jacket matches your new van?" Ben said, a small smile tugging at his lips.

"Yes, and I couldn't decide if that was corny or cute."

Ben raised one hand as though to touch her face, then dropped it back to his side.

"It's cute," he said. "Way cool, as Eagle would say."

"Well, what more could a person want than to be way cool?"

"Yeah."

They stood there for a timeless moment, looking deep into each other's eyes, oblivious to the wind and the cold. They didn't move or hardly breathe. Then thunder rumbled, the sudden noise jerking them from the hazy mist that seemed to have swirled around and encased them in a private place.

Ben cleared his throat. "We'd better get going. I think it's going to rain on your new van."

"Life has a way of raining on parades at times," Laurel said quietly. "I'll meet you at the house and we'll get my mother's report on Grandfather."

Big drops of rain began to fall, and Laurel turned and hurried to get inside the van at the same time Ben strode to his vehicle.

"Goodbye, Ben," Laurel whispered. "Goodbye, stranger."

At the Windsong home Jane came out carrying an umbrella and gushed over Laurel's new purchase. Ben pulled into the driveway behind Laurel, and she scooted under the umbrella with her mother to go to the open window of Ben's Tahoe.

"I just wondered how you found Grandfather, Jane?" Ben said.

"He wasn't home," Jane said. "You know he never locks his door, so I took the food I'd brought him inside and put it in the refrigerator. His truck wasn't there, so he'd gone farther than just on a walk. I stopped by to say hello to Dove, then checked at Grandfather's again after that, but he still wasn't there. I have no idea where he went."

"Okay," Ben said. "Thanks."

"Would you like to come in, Ben?" Jane said. "I made a big pot of vegetable soup we could all share for dinner later."

"No. Thanks, but no," Ben said. "I'm going to go out to the rez and see if Grandfather's back, then settle in by a warm fire at home. It looks like we're in for a lengthy rain."

"It will cut short the tourist traffic to town if this wind whips all the leaves off the trees," Jane said, frowning. "That's not good. Things could get quiet until there's enough snow for skiing. That will take a nasty bite out of the revenue we all count on."

"Well, maybe this storm will move on through in a hurry," Ben said. "I'd better go."

"You and Laurel certainly picked out a nice vehicle for her," Jane said, smiling. "You're a good team."

"I'm cold," Laurel said, then took off at a run for the house.

"See you, Jane," Ben said, then pressed the button to close the window on his vehicle and backed out of the driveway.

"Those two," Jane said, starting toward the house, "look as though they just came from the dentist instead of having a nice day in Flagstaff together. Oh, dear." She gave Laurel's van a friendly pat, then went on to the house.

It was raining harder by the time Ben arrived at Grandfather's trailer. Dove was coming down the three wooden steps leading to the front door and waved to Ben as he drove up. She ran to where he stopped and slid onto the passenger seat, pulling the door closed behind her.

"Wet, cold and windy," she said, shivering. "The pretty leaves don't stand a chance, and that's not good for the revenue of the shop owners of Willow Valley. The tourists won't be back until it's time to ski."

"Yep," Ben said, frowning. "Grandfather still isn't home? There's no light on in his trailer."

"No, he's not there," Dove said. "Jane told me she'd taken him some food, but he wasn't home. I wanted to see if he was back yet. I ran into Cadillac in town earlier and he said he saw Grandfather on the interstate in his rusty old truck and he took the south exit."

"South?" Ben said, looking over at Dove. "He was headed for Phoenix? That doesn't make sense, Dove. Grandfather hates to go to Phoenix. I can't even remember the last time he went down there."

"I know." Dove shifted in her seat to face Ben. "What if he was going to see a doctor? He has *not* been feeling well."

"He goes to Doc Willie on the rare occasion that he sees a doctor at all," Ben said. "Why would he go...unless..."

"Unless he doesn't want to take the chance that anyone here knows how sick he really is."

"Let's not jump to conclusions," Ben said,

shaking his head. "There are other reasons to go to Phoenix."

"Name one thing Grandfather would go down there for."

Ben opened his mouth to reply, then snapped it closed when he realized he didn't have an answer. His shoulders slumped and he sighed.

"What are we going to do, Ben?" Dove said.

"There's not a lot we can do. Grandfather won't talk until he's ready. We'll stick to our plan. You, Laurel and I will keep checking in on him and compare notes."

"Okay," Dove said. "But I'm just so worried about him and I feel helpless."

"Yeah, I know."

"Jane told me that you and Laurel went to Flagstaff so Laurel could buy a vehicle. Did she get something?"

"A Dodge minivan. The smaller one," Ben said, shifting his gaze to the front window. "It's red. Matches her jacket. They shined it all up for her, but now it's getting wet."

"Did you two have a nice day together?" Dove said, leaning slightly toward him.

Ben laughed, a short bark of sound that held no humor. "I wouldn't say that. Not even close."

"What happened?"

Using as few words as possible, Ben related what

had come to light about Laurel's leaving Willow Valley ten years before.

Dove's eyes widened. "You didn't hear her tell you that she'd gotten the scholarship to Virginia and that was the only reason she was going so far away? You didn't hear that?"

"No."

"So you didn't say you'd wait for her if she went to college closer to home? Oh, God, Ben, this is awful, just terrible. You two could have worked out a compromise about Laurel wanting to be a psychologist and... I can't believe this." She paused. "Okay, okay, I'm calming down. You both know the truth now, so you can repair the damage that was done."

"No, Dove. It's too late for that. Ten years is a long time. Laurel and I are different people now, strangers. We can't turn back the clock and pretend— I don't want to discuss this any further. You'd better get home before the roads are thick with mud from this rain."

"But..."

"Go on, Dove."

"Navajos are so darn stubborn," Dove said. "When you don't want to talk about something... I swear, you'd think you were the one who is really related to Grandfather, not me. You drive me nuts."

"Oh, yeah? What about you? Every time I ask

you what you plan to do after Eagle graduates, you just dust me off and say you're fine as you are."

"I *am* fine as I am."

"You're a stubborn Navajo, Dove Clearwater."

"I'm going home," she said, opening the door and leaving the vehicle.

Ben watched until Dove drove away, then stared at Grandfather's dark trailer for another long moment before heading for home, his mood as dark as the rain-laden clouds in the sky.

"And that's what happened," Laurel said, absently stirring the soup in her bowl as she sat across the kitchen table from her mother.

"It was all a misunderstanding," Jane said incredulously. "You and Ben each came to the wrong conclusions because... Oh, Laurel, this is so...so..."

"Sad," Laurel said quietly.

"Yes, honey, but now you both know the truth. No one was betrayed. Promises weren't broken. It was a simple but heartbreaking case of lack of proper communication. You and Ben can pick up the pieces and—"

"No," Laurel said. "It's too late. Ten years too late. We're strangers now."

"But you're still in love with him, Laurel."

"I'm in love with the Ben I knew ten years ago. I

don't even know the man he's become. Besides, he's not in love with me, which is a point that should not be forgotten. Could we change the subject, please? There's nothing more to be said about this."

"Your stubborn Navajo side is showing, Miss," Jane said, frowning. "You're reminding me of your father at the moment."

"Fine," Laurel said, lifting her chin.

"Eat your soup." Jane paused. "I really like your vehicle."

"Me, too, except..." Laurel threw up her hands. "To top off this really crummy, awful, sad, sad day, it even rained on my pretty new red van. And wearing a red jacket while driving a red van is definitely corny, not cute. And I'm going to go to bed and cry for twenty-two years. Good night, Mother."

After tossing and turning in bed for what seemed like an eternity, Ben finally dozed off in a light, troubled sleep, only to have the telephone ring and jar him back awake. He fumbled in the dark for the receiver.

"Sheriff Skeeter," he said groggily.

"Sheriff? This is Bobby. Sorry to wake you."

Ben snapped on the lamp next to the bed and sat up as he heard the voice of one of his deputies.

"What's the problem, Bobby?" he said, his grip on the receiver tightening.

"There's been another break-in at one of the empty summer homes. The Madison place. I'm here now and...this one is different, Sheriff. It doesn't even make sense because... Could you come out here? I think you'd better see this, not just read my report on it in the morning."

"I'm on my way, Bobby," Ben said, tossing back the blankets on the bed.

Chapter Six

To save time, Ben had pulled on the same clothes he'd worn to Flagstaff rather than bothering with his official uniform. It was still raining as he drove into the driveway at the Madison home, and the wind was blowing even more fiercely. He made a dash for the door of the house. Bobby's patrol car was in the driveway above where Ben had parked, and another one was in front of the large house.

Inside the nicely furnished house Ben was immediately greeted by Bobby, who told him that another deputy, Mike, was outside checking for footprints, which probably wouldn't produce any results because of the rain.

"Yeah, okay," Ben said. "So what's so different about this break-in, Bobby?"

"I'll show you," Bobby said, starting across the spacious living room. "He came in through the kitchen window, smashed it and undid the lock, just like the other break-ins."

In the gleaming kitchen Ben frowned as Bobby swept one arm in the direction of the floor beneath the double sink below the broken window.

"See?" Bobby said. "He stacked everything up. VCR, DVD player, microwave, all that stuff, but it's still sitting there. And look there on the floor. That's blood, Sheriff, but there's no blood around the window or on any of the glass, so he didn't cut himself coming in. Also, the canister set from the counter is broken there on the floor, and the toaster and coffeemaker are hanging off the counter by the cords."

Ben pushed his Stetson up with a thumb and folded his arms across his chest as he studied the scene before him. He nodded slowly.

"Okay. Tell me what you're thinking, Bobby," he said finally.

"Well, sir, it looks to me like a fight took place in here. There were two guys, not one, and for some reason they got into an argument and duked it out. Why they left the loot behind, I really don't know.

"There's quite a bit of blood. I'd guess maybe a bloody nose? I'd hate to think it was worse—you know, a knife fight or whatever. I don't know, Sheriff Skeeter. This doesn't make much sense to me."

"Don't sell yourself short, Bobby," Ben said. "I think you've sized things up pretty well. There's obviously two people involved in these break-ins, and something happened in here tonight to cause them to go after each other. Let's get some samples of this blood and dust for fingerprints, like we did with the other houses, which got us nowhere."

"Yes, sir," Bobby said.

Another deputy came into the kitchen wearing a yellow slicker that was dripping water.

"Any luck, Mike?" Ben said.

"No, sir. Any footprints there might have been out there are washed away by the rain. Man, that wind is still whipping the leaves from the trees. That is going to cause such money problems for the merchants in town."

"Yeah," Ben said, staring again at the equipment piled on the floor. "Okay. Mike, find something to board up that window with. Bobby, you get samples of the blood and dust for prints. I'll call the Madisons in the morning and tell them what happened. No sense in disturbing their sleep, because what's done is done."

The two deputies nodded.

"I want the details about this break-in kept quiet," Ben said. "I'll release a statement to the paper that there's been another break-in and we're following several leads and blah, blah, blah. I don't want anything leaking about the blood, the fact that we think there were two guys in here, none of that."

"Got it," Mike said, then frowned. "Why?"

"Because," Ben said, "I want these two yo-yos to think we were too dumb to figure out there was a fight in here. It will appear that we've decided he cut himself on the jagged glass coming in through the window. I'll fill in the other guys when they come on duty tomorrow.

"Without being obvious about it, keep an eye out for anyone with fresh bruises, probably on their face, possibly on their knuckles. If this blood is from a nose, that nose is swollen and broken noses cause black eyes more often than not."

"But if there's a knife involved?" Mike said.

"Then it won't be that easy to detect. I'll check with Doc Willie to see if anyone came in with a knife wound but— No, the knife thing isn't working for me. Think about the stuff they're taking. These aren't big-time operators. They're ripping off cheap goods that are easy to sell. I'm betting it's kids, teenagers, and they slugged it out over...over something."

"Makes sense," Mike said, nodding.

"I'll be at the high school in the morning, just hanging out by the front door as the students go in," Ben continued. "I'll get there early enough to see the kids getting off the bus from the rez, too. After class starts, I'll check with the principal and see who's absent if I didn't spot what I'm looking for."

"Oh," Bobby said, nodding. "That's really smart." He laughed. "Which is why you're the sheriff and I'm one of the deputies who takes orders from you."

"You did a fine job tonight, Bobby," Ben said. "You, too, Mike. I think we're definitely closer to catching these jerks. I didn't really believe there were two of them because the stuff taken was small, easily carried by one person." He chuckled. "I blew that one. Okay. I'm out of here. Remember, mum's the word on the details we're not divulging. Any questions?"

"Just one," Mike said. "Did Laurel want a red vehicle? Or was that the only color they had on the lot for that size van?"

"Man, oh, man," Ben said, shaking his head. "You gotta love living in Willow Valley. Sneeze and ten people say bless you. Try this— Laurel bought a red van because it matched her jacket."

"Whoa," Bobby said. "That is really a girl thing,

isn't it? I will never understand women. Not even if I live as long as Grandfather."

"I was kidding," Ben said, shaking his head. "She wanted red, she bought red, then realized it matched her jacket. But as far as understanding women? It isn't going to happen." He paused. "Have either of you heard anything about Grandfather's health?"

Both deputies shook their heads.

"All right," Ben said. "Write up your reports on this break-in before you go off duty after you finish up here. I'll see you later."

"Yes, sir," the pair said in unison.

"Good work tonight, gentlemen," Ben said, then strode from the room.

The next morning, when Ben leaned against the wall next to the front doors of the high school, he hunched his shoulders against a chill wind. It had stopped raining, and a pale blue sky with a smattering of clouds that appeared as though they might still have rain to offer made the day rather gloomy, which matched Ben's mood.

He hated the idea that a couple of the students who were just beginning to arrive at the school had messed up their lives by breaking into the summer homes, Ben thought. But all the evidence pointed toward kids out to get some extra money.

He'd spoken to the principal upon arriving to let the man know why the sheriff would be stationed by the front door. The same principal who had been in charge when he and Laurel had gone to school here.

Man, this building was ancient and was really showing the wear and tear of time. It needed to be refurbished from top to bottom. Better yet, a new high school should be built from scratch. Well, that wasn't going to happen because there just wasn't that kind of money in Willow Valley and the rez.

High school, Ben mused, nodding at a stream of students who looked at him questioningly as they strolled into the building. Those had been the days when he and Laurel had believed that everything they planned would come true. It was as simple as that. They wanted it, it would happen. They'd been so much in love, had their future life together all figured out and...

Don't go there, Skeeter, he told himself. It served no purpose to dwell on the past, on the might-have-beens, on what was supposed to have taken place. But, God, to think that it had all fallen apart because he and Laurel hadn't communicated well on the subject of her wanting to be a psychologist— Forget it. Just forget it.

"Hi, Sheriff Skeeter," a pretty young girl said. "Are you doing a homeland security check or something?"

"Or something," Ben said, smiling. "Nothing fancy. Just routine."

"That's what they say on TV," the girl said, "but it never is just routine. You've never stood by the door like this before."

"I'm just reminiscing about the days I spent here when I was your age," Ben said.

"Really? This building is that old? You went to high school here?"

"Well, that sure made my day," Ben said, shaking his head. "You'd better go on in. It's cold out here."

"Okay," she said. "Did you see how many of the pretty leaves were blown off the trees? My folks are really upset about it because the tourists won't have anything to come see. Grim. Brrr. I'm freezing. Bye."

Ben nodded, then straightened and narrowed his eyes as the bus from the reservation pulled up in front and the students began to clamor off the rickety vehicle.

As much as he hated to admit it, Ben thought, he was betting his buck that the break-ins had been pulled off by kids from the rez. The level of poverty out there was getting worse instead of better, and the temptation to break the law to put money in pockets was high.

A dozen Navajo students glanced at Ben, then went inside, with a steady stream behind them coming up the cracked sidewalk.

Ben took a step forward and his heart began to

pound as he saw Dove's brother, Eagle, stop dead in his tracks and look around frantically. Eagle, who had two black eyes and a puffy nose, turned and ran back down the walkway.

"Eagle," Ben yelled. "Hold it right there."

Eagle kept running and Ben took off after him. Eagle was fast, but Ben was faster and caught the boy at the far end of the school yard, grabbing him by the back of his jacket, spinning him around and pushing him chest-first against the chain-link fence. A group of students stopped and stared at what was taking place.

"Get your hands off me," Eagle said.

Ben turned Eagle around and flattened one hand on the boy's chest. Normally Eagle Clearwater was a good-looking kid who had a bevy of girls trying to get his attention. Today, though, there was nothing handsome about his beat-up face.

"Take it easy, Eagle," Ben said. "I just want to ask you a couple questions."

"I'm going to be late for class," Eagle said sullenly. "You going to do my detention for me?"

"What happened to your face?" Ben said, keeping his hand splayed on Eagle's chest.

"I ran into the edge of my bedroom door."

"It that what you told Dove?" Ben said.

"Yeah, and she believed me."

"Well, I don't," Ben said. "I missed seeing the

rest of the boys from the rez get off the bus because you took off. Who else looks like you do this morning, Eagle?"

"I don't know what you're talking about," Eagle said, staring down at the ground. "I didn't see that my bedroom door was half open because it was dark. Okay? Can I go now?"

"Nope." Ben sighed. "Aw, man, Eagle, what were you thinking? You've got straight A's, you're headed for a career in the Army and you throw it all away by breaking into the summer homes?"

"I didn't, Sheriff Skeeter," Eagle said, meeting Ben's gaze. "I swear to you I didn't do that." His puffy, discolored eyes filled with tears. "I'm graduating in the spring, have my future all laid out. And besides, I would never do something so crummy and upset Dove. I love her. She's the best, you know?"

"I know," Ben said quietly, crossing his arms over his chest. "She's so proud of you, Eagle. Okay, buddy, what really happened to your face?"

Eagle shook his head. "I can't tell you."

"Fine," Ben said, his jaw tightening. "Then I'll tell you. You and one of your pals have been doing the break-ins at the summer homes. All of them. Last night, for some reason, you and said chum got into a fight about whatever at the Madison place and beat each other to a pulp. Who is he, Eagle? I'll find out, you know, by looking for someone who has a messed-up face like yours."

"You've got it all wrong," Eagle said, shaking his head and sniffling.

"Well, set me straight. Here, or down at the station. Your choice."

The school bell rang, and the students who had gathered to watch the excitement between Sheriff Skeeter and Eagle Clearwater took off at a run for the front door of the building.

"I didn't do anything wrong," Eagle said.

"Okay, let's go," Ben said, taking Eagle's arm.

"You're not going to call Dove, are you?"

"Yep," Ben said, opening the rear door of the patrol car. "She's your legal guardian and should be there before I question you any further."

"Oh, man, oh, man," Eagle said, sliding onto the back seat of the car. "You just don't understand."

"No, I sure don't," Ben said wearily.

The small brick building housing the Willow Valley Sheriff's Department was in about the same shape as the high school. It was old, the heating was iffy at best and the metal desks and leather chairs were ancient. The rear of the building had four holding cells with rusted bars. Ben placed Eagle in one of the cells.

In his twelve-feet-square office Ben sank onto his cracked leather chair behind his dented desk and called the Clearwater home. No one answered. He drummed his fingers on the desk, trying to imagine where Dove might have gone so early in the morning.

To check on Grandfather? he wondered. Did she come into town with some of her crafts to place in the shops? The stores weren't open yet. Okay, what if she brought the stuff in with the intention of having breakfast at the Windsong Café while waiting for the stores to open for business? It was worth a try.

Ben dialed the number he knew by heart.

"Windsong Café," Laurel said cheerfully, picking up the telephone halfway through the third ring.

"It's Ben, Laurel," he said, once again recognizing her voice. "Is Dove there by any chance? If she is, don't let on that I asked."

"Yes, she's here," Laurel said, frowning as she lowered her voice. "She's having some tea and toast while she's waiting for the shops to… What's wrong, Ben? Why are you looking for Dove?"

"I need her to come to the station," Ben said. "Look, is it really busy in the café this morning? This is going to be tough on Dove, and it would be good if you were with her for moral support. Can you leave there?"

"Yes, of course, if Dove needs me," Laurel said,

making certain no one could hear what she was saying. "But you're scaring me to death, Ben. What's going on?"

"It's Eagle," Ben said. "I think he's in trouble. Big time."

"Oh, no, no, there must be some mistake," Laurel said, shaking her head.

"Just get Dove over here, would you?" Ben said.

"Yes. Right away."

"Thanks, Laurel," Ben said, then hung up the receiver.

Laurel took her mother aside and explained what had transpired during the telephone conversation with Ben.

"Ben wants me to be with Dove because this is going to be so upsetting for her," Laurel whispered.

"Of course," Jane said. "But I can't believe that Eagle has done anything wrong. I'm going to be a wreck until I hear from you. Go, sweetheart. Don't worry about things here at the café. We'll do fine."

Laurel nodded, then hurried to where Dove was sitting and slid into the booth across the table from her.

"Taking a break?" Dove said, smiling.

"Not exactly," Laurel said. "Dove, Ben just called and… Stay calm. Something has taken place that makes it appear that…that Eagle is in trouble."

Dove's eyes widened. "What kind of trouble?"

"I don't know," Laurel said, shrugging. "You and I are going to go find out. Come on. I'll drive."

"Ben has Eagle at the sheriff's office?" Dove said, sliding out of the booth. "This is crazy. Eagle went to school. I offered to drive him because I was coming into town, but he said he'd rather ride the bus. I guess it's not cool to be seen being dropped off by your big sister and— Oh, God, Laurel, what kind of trouble?"

"Come on," Laurel said, starting to walk away.

"I have to pay for my tea and toast," Dove said, not moving.

"Forget that," Laurel said, retracing her steps and grabbing Dove by the arm.

"What's happenin'?" Cadillac said, turning on his stool at the counter.

"More coffee, Cadillac?" Jane said, causing him to spin back around to face her.

Laurel grabbed her red jacket from the office off the hallway leading to the back door, and a few minutes later she and Dove were driving toward Ben's building.

"I don't understand this at all," Dove said, shaking her head.

"We'll find out what's going on," Laurel said, her hold on the steering wheel tightening.

She drove three blocks down and one block over to the shabby brick building, then she and Dove rushed through the door and straight to Ben's office inside. He stood as they entered.

"Ben?" Dove said.

"Sit down, please," he said, sweeping one arm toward the two chairs fronting his desk.

"No," Dove said. "Is Eagle here?"

"Yes. Dove, sit down," Ben said.

Dove sank onto one of the chairs and Laurel sat on the other one.

Ben sighed. "Look, the evidence we have against Eagle is circumstantial, nothing concrete at this point, but there are questions that need answers. I can't talk to him without you being with him, Dove, because he's underage." He paused. "Dove, did you see Eagle's face this morning?"

"His face?" she said, sliding to the edge of her chair and leaning toward Ben. "Yes, I saw it. He got up in the night to get a drink of water and his bedroom door was halfway open. He didn't see it in the dark and slammed right into it. I think his nose might be broken because his eyes turned black and— Why are you asking me about Eagle's face, Ben?"

"You didn't hear anything in the night?" Ben said. "He must have made some noise. Banging into a door that hard would hurt like hell."

"No, I didn't hear a thing."

"Did you see any blood on what he wears to bed?" Ben said.

"Well, no, he was already dressed when... Where is Eagle, Ben?" Dove said. "What have you done with him?"

"He's in a holding cell in the back and—"

Dove jumped to her feet. "You put my baby brother in a cell?"

Laurel pulled on Dove's arm and got her to sit back down.

"Ben," Laurel said. "Could you get to the point a little faster? What is it that you believe Eagle has done? Since when is it against the law to get a broken nose by banging into a door in the dark?"

Ben raised both hands in a gesture of peace, then related what had been discovered at the Madison home the previous night.

"And you think my brother and someone else are the ones who have been breaking into the summer homes?" Dove said, her voice rising. "Benjamin Skeeter, you are out of your mind."

"I sincerely hope so, Dove," Ben said. "But I need a feasible explanation for the condition of Eagle's face this morning."

"He gave you one!" Dove yelled.

"I can't buy it, Dove," Ben said quietly. "You

would have heard him in the night if it really happened the way he's telling it. Plus, I can't picture him wiping up every drop of blood at that hour."

"Yes, he would." Dove pressed one hand to her forehead. "No, he wouldn't. Oh, God."

"Okay. Let's get him in here and see what he has to say," Ben said.

Dove nodded jerkily and Laurel squeezed her best friend's shoulder. Within minutes Ben returned with Eagle and another chair, which he set next to Dove. Eagle slouched onto it, crossed his arms over his chest and glowered at a spot on the wall.

"From the top, Eagle," Ben said, sitting back down behind his desk. "What happened to your face?"

"I told you already," Eagle mumbled.

"I don't believe you," Ben said.

"Tough," Eagle said.

"Eagle Clearwater," Dove said, "you sit up straight in that chair and answer Ben's—answer Sheriff Skeeter's questions. He thinks you and someone who was with you are guilty of breaking into all those summer homes. This isn't funny, Eagle. This is very serious and you've got to tell the truth. Right now."

Eagle pushed himself upward in the chair. "I didn't steal anything. I didn't break into any of those houses. I swear I didn't."

"Were you at the Madison home last night, Eagle?" Ben said quietly.

"I... It's not like you think," Eagle said.

"Were you there?" Ben said.

"Yeah, but..."

"Dear heaven," Dove said, pressing trembling fingertips to her lips.

"Dove, no, wait," Eagle said. "I didn't steal anything. I wouldn't do that, you know I wouldn't. I was just trying to... I didn't want..." He shook his head as tears filled his eyes. "Forget it."

"Who are you protecting, Eagle?" Laurel said gently. "Loyalty and a code of honor are fine, but not at the expense of destroying your own future.

"You went to the Madison house to attempt to stop someone you care about from robbing yet another summer home. Right?

"You're a good friend, Eagle, but you've done all you can do for that person. He has to pay the consequences for his own choices, don't you see? If he doesn't, he'll continue on as he is, believing that his actions are fine as long as he doesn't get caught. Do you want to be responsible for him having that mind-set?"

A heavy silence fell in the room.

There was the answer, Ben thought, staring at Laurel, who was staring at Eagle. Laurel had nailed it. Damn, she was a fine psychologist, and he was so proud of her at this moment he could burst his buttons. He'd been afraid that Eagle had done something so stupid that his future plans were blown to hell, but Laurel... Oh, man, he loved that woman.

Eagle sniffled. "I tried to stop him. I really did. He's been bragging to me about the money he's going to get from selling the stuff he took from the houses and I told him he would get caught, go to jail, but he wouldn't listen to me.

"He said he was doing the Madison place last night, and I went there and we got into a fight because I said he wasn't taking anything out of that window, and he broke my nose. But I sort of busted his arm and... I didn't mean to break his arm, but when I shoved him back through the window, he landed hard on the ground with his arm under him, then he got up and just took off."

"Who is he, Eagle?" Ben said softly.

"My...my cousin, Yazzie Slowtalker," Eagle said.

"Oh, no," Dove said. "Aunt Bethany is going to be devastated."

"I know that, Dove," Eagle said. "Aunt Bethany is a cool lady and I like her a lot, you know? She's our mom's sister and she tells me great stories about our mom and dad and she works so hard to buy food and stuff for all of them in that house and it's never enough for Yazzie, never, ever enough.

"I tried to get through to him, Dove, I did, but he wouldn't listen to me. So I snuck out last night and went to the Madison house and... I thought I could fix things somehow but... I'm sorry. I made a big mess of the whole number and I even broke Yazzie's arm and... I'm sorry, Dove, I really am and..."

"Shh, honey, what you did was wonderful," Dove said. "My heart is filled with such pride over what you attempted to do."

"Really?" Eagle said.

"Really, *sitsili,* my younger brother," Dove said, smiling at him. "May we leave now, Ben? I want Doc Willie to take a look at Eagle's nose. We'll walk down the block to his office. Okay?"

Ben nodded. "I'll need a statement from Eagle, but we'll get it later. We'll find Yazzie and wrap this thing up." He got to his feet. "Eagle, I'm proud to know you. You go on with Dove now."

Laurel stood and hugged Dove, then Eagle. She watched as they left Ben's office.

"You're a helluva fine psychologist, Laurel," Ben said. "You've got a gift, a sixth sense or something. You zeroed right in on the truth, while I was still heartsick over what could happen to Eagle if he'd really gotten so far off the proper path. Yeah, you're very good at your chosen profession."

Laurel's head snapped around and she looked at

Ben as the color drained from her face. "No, I'm not. I'm not. I've known Eagle since he was born. That's why I knew he couldn't be guilty. It has nothing to do with my training. Nothing at all."

Ben frowned. "I've known that kid since he was born, too, but I thought he might have done it. Why are you diminishing your abilities as a psychologist? Take credit where it's due. You're good, very good."

"No...I'm not," Laurel said, taking several steps backward. "I don't want—I don't want to discuss this further. I'm grateful that Eagle is innocent and... I've got to get back to the café."

"Laurel, wait a minute," Ben said, coming around to the front of his desk. "What's going on with you? You're pale, you're even trembling. Talk to me. You just did a fantastic thing in this room and you're acting so strange. Laurel?"

"No. No," she said, shaking her head. "I have to go. I left my mother short of help at the café. I have to go."

Laurel turned and ran from the room. Ben frowned deeply and hooked one hand over the back of his neck as he looked at the doorway Laurel had fled through. He walked slowly to his desk chair and sank onto it heavily.

The mystery of the robberies of the summer homes had been solved, he thought. He would have gotten the truth out of Eagle eventually by going over and over the questions and hammering away at the kid until he spilled it. But Laurel had done an incredible got-it-in-one.

Now, didn't that sound like a happy ending? Except, of course, for Yazzie. And his mom, who deserved better than the news Sheriff Skeeter was going to have to tell her. But the crime spree was over and the fine citizens of Willow Valley and the rez could sleep easy tonight.

But *he* wouldn't. No way. Because he was now facing a new mystery—Laurel Windsong's bizarre behavior when he'd praised her on her fine abilities as a psychologist. She'd fallen apart right before his eyes, then gone running back to the Windsong Café and her mother.

Just like the way she'd come running home to Willow Valley from Virginia.

Chapter Seven

It was nearly eleven o'clock that night before Ben was able to head home. He was tired, more emotionally exhausted than physically, and his stomach grumbled because he'd been unable to take the time to eat either lunch or dinner.

He'd found Yazzie Slowtalker curled up in a wooden shed behind his house, cradling the broken arm he'd suffered when Eagle had shoved him out the window of the Madison house. Yazzie had been cold, hungry and in pain and had burst into tears when he saw his mother and Sheriff Skeeter. He quickly confessed to all the break-ins of the summer homes, saying he just wanted to get some money so he could leave the reservation after he graduated from high school in the spring.

Bethany Slowtalker had hugged her son and, with tears streaming down her face, told him she'd stand by his side through the legal ordeal yet to come. Ben had hurried home to change into a fresh uniform, then driven the pair over to Prescott, where charges were filed against Yazzie and he was placed in the juvenile detention center. A public defender was assigned to his case and the young woman said she'd drive Bethany back to Willow Valley.

Upon returning to town, Ben gave a statement to the newspaper saying the person responsible for the break-ins had been apprehended but because he was a minor his name was not being released. Ben knew full well that by then everyone in town and on the rez knew the whole story of Yazzie's crime spree and Eagle's attempt to stop his cousin, but at least the information had not come from the sheriff's office.

Ben went to Dove's to get Eagle's official statement, realized it was too late in the day to check on Grandfather, then returned to the office to type up the endless reports necessary to complete the file.

"Home, food, bed," Ben mumbled as he approached his house.

He turned into the long driveway that kept the

house hidden from the road, then frowned as he saw that the sensor lights he'd installed were glowing in the distance. Deciding that an animal from the woods had no doubt wandered in front of the house and triggered the lights, Ben stiffened in shock when he saw Laurel's red van. He parked next to it, and she got out and met him at the side of his vehicle.

"Hello," Ben said. "I don't mean to be rude, Laurel, but why are you here? How long have you been waiting for me to show up? No, back up. Why are you here?"

"I had to come, Ben," Laurel said. "I came as soon as I got off work at the café. I knew you'd get home eventually. You've had a long day."

"Yeah. What—I mean why—" Ben sighed. "Look, I'm bushed and I'm starving to death. There's obviously something on your mind, so why don't you come in while I get some food in me."

"Yes, all right. Thank you."

Inside the house, Ben turned on lights, locked his gun in a box on the closet shelf, set his Stetson next to the box then headed for the kitchen.

"Your home is absolutely beautiful," Laurel said, glancing around as she followed him. "It's really lovely, Ben, and just the way you used to describe it and draw all those pictures of it so many years ago when you saw it so clearly in your mind."

"Yep," Ben said, opening the refrigerator and pulling things out. "Are you hungry?"

"No."

"Well, sit down at the table while I make myself a sandwich, then you can tell me why you camped out here waiting for me."

A short time later Ben sat opposite Laurel, a huge sandwich on a plate and a tall glass of milk next to it. He took a bite of the sandwich and raised his eyebrows at Laurel as he chewed, indicating he was ready for her to speak. Laurel clutched her hands tightly in her lap and met Ben's gaze.

"I came to apologize for my behavior in your office this morning," Laurel said, her voice not quite steady. "You paid me a very nice compliment when you said you felt I was a good psychologist because of the way I approached Eagle, and I acted like a total idiot. I'm very sorry for my behavior, Ben. I knew I wouldn't sleep tonight until I spoke to you. So here I am and I am very, very sorry." She started to rise. "There."

"Sit," Ben said, pointing to the chair Laurel was about to leave.

She plunked back down.

"So, okay, you're sorry you acted the way you did," he said, no readable expression on his face. "But I think I'm due more than that, Laurel. My question is, why did you behave that way? My guess is that it has something to do with your sudden re-appearance in Willow Valley. Don't you believe it's time you told me what's really going on with you?"

"No," Laurel said, shaking her head. "I'm not ready to talk about it, Ben. I haven't even told Dove, and she hasn't pushed me on the subject. I have some...issues to work through and..."

"Issues?" Ben interrupted. "Oh, now there's a great shrink word. Chalk it all up to issues. What's next? You need to get in touch with your inner child? Give me a break." He finished the milk and thudded the glass back onto the table. "Hell."

"This was a mistake," Laurel said, getting to her feet. "You're tired and I know you must be upset about Yazzie. All I focused on was what I needed to do so I could sleep tonight and I didn't think about the shape you might be in this late. Well, I'm sorry again, Ben. Now I'm guilty of being self-centered. I'm batting a thousand here. I'll leave you in peace."

"Laurel," Ben said wearily, "I haven't had much peace of mind since you left me ten years ago. Now? Whoa, look who's back in Willow Valley, folks, with absolutely no explanation as to why. And to top off this nice emotional cake that's being baked, we discover that what happened ten years ago was a lack of proper communication." He shook his head.

"Proper communication. There's another shrink phrase, huh? A real beaut."

"Ben..."

"What?" he said, rising and going to where she stood. "What else do you want to say to me, Laurel? You know what really fries me? You're *still* not *communicating*. You won't explain why you came running home from Virginia, why you freaked when I made reference to your skills as a psychologist.

"You're back in town, making me want you until I ache, making me relive all the memories of what we shared, and you're keeping so many damn secrets it's a wonder you can even function."

"I..."

"Well, I know one truth about you, Laurel Windsong," Ben said, a rough edge to his voice as he gripped her shoulders. "When I kissed you by the lake, you responded to me, totally, absolutely, holding nothing back. You desire me as much as I do you. And that is a fact. There's no secret about it, Laurel."

And with that, Ben pulled her close and captured her mouth with his in a searing kiss.

Laurel stiffened and her eyes widened in shock, but in the next instant she melted into the kiss, wrapping her arms around Ben's neck and allowing her lashes to drift down as she savored the taste, the aroma, the kiss that was Ben.

The draining events of the day dissipated as Ben lost himself in the kiss.

He'd come home from a grueling day and Laurel had been waiting for him, he thought hazily, just the way it was supposed to be.

She'd sat with him while he'd had something to eat, and now he was holding her in his arms before they went upstairs to their bed to make sweet, slow love, just the way it was supposed to be.

Laurel was here, just the way it was supposed to be.

Ben raised his head a fraction of an inch to speak close to Laurel's moist lips.

"I want you," he said, his voice husky. "I want to make love with you so damn much, Laurel."

"I want you, too, Ben," she said. "I do. I…" She sighed and eased away from him. "No, I'm doing it again. I'm centered on what *I* want, and that's not fair, not right at all. I have nothing to offer you, Ben. My life is a confused jumble, a total mess right now. I don't know what I'm doing or where I'm going or…" She shook her head. "I'd better leave before— I'm sorry."

"Would you quit apologizing for stuff every two seconds?" he said.

"I have to because I keep making mistakes."

"Is it a mistake to want me, Laurel?" he said, dragging a restless hand through his hair. "Is it? No, because I want you, too. Now. Tonight. No promises.

No regrets. No talk about tomorrow. Just tonight. Us. Together. How could that possibly be wrong?"

"I don't know if... I can't think straight."

"Laurel, I closed the door when we came in here. I shut out the world beyond this house, this moment. No one exists but the two of us."

Laurel nodded slowly. "No promises. No regrets. Just tonight."

"*Our* night." Ben framed Laurel's face in his hands and looked directly into her eyes. "It's up to you. Say yes or no. The decision is yours to make."

There *was* no decision to make, nothing to ponder, weigh and measure, Laurel thought as heat suffused her. She wanted to make love with Ben so much. Tonight. Their night. No promises. No regrets. She refused to think, she was just going to feel, savor, give herself this stolen moment out of time like a precious gift to be cherished. All she had to do was say...

"Yes," she whispered. "Oh, Ben, yes. Just this night, this one night. Yes."

A groan rumbled in Ben's chest as he kissed Laurel deeply, then broke the kiss to encircle her shoulders with his arm and lead her from the kitchen. They went up the stairs to Ben's room. The storm had passed through and the moon and the sparkling stars cast a silvery glow through the skylight above Ben's king-size bed.

Ben flung back the blankets on the bed, then extended one hand to Laurel in a last gesture to allow her to change her mind. She looked at his large hand, understanding what he was doing, then met his gaze as a soft womanly smile formed on her lips. She placed her hand in his.

Ben wrapped his fingers gently around hers, then closed his eyes for a moment to allow the anticipation of what was to come to consume him, touch his heart, his mind, his very soul.

By unspoken agreement they shed their clothes quickly, urgently, letting them fall where they may. They stood naked before the other with no apprehension, sweeping their gazes over the other, seeing the subtle changes that nature had brought as they'd matured.

"You're beautiful, Laurel Windsong," Ben said, his voice husky with building passion.

"And you are magnificent," she said, her voice hushed with awe.

Ben stepped behind her, and with hands that trembled slightly, he undid the thick braid of her hair. He sifted his fingers through it, watching the ebony tresses glide like a silken waterfall. He turned her toward him and floated her hair over her breasts, his heart thundering.

"Nizhonigo nanina," he said.

"*Ahehee*," Laurel whispered.

"No, don't thank me. You *do* walk in beauty."

Ben lifted her into his arms, placed her in the center of the bed and followed her down, catching his weight on his forearms. He kissed her, parting her lips, delving his tongue into the sweet darkness beyond, where she met his tongue with hers, stroking, dueling, dancing, causing heated desire to rush throughout them.

He brushed her hair aside to seek and find one of her breasts, laving the nipple with his tongue, then moving to the other one as she splayed her hands on his back, savoring the feel of his bunching muscles beneath her palms. He left the rich bounty of her breasts to move lower, trailing a ribbon of kisses along her dewy skin. A purr of pleasure escaped from Laurel's lips.

It was familiar, evoking memories that refused to stay in the shadows of their minds. Yet it was new and rich and wonderful, as well. They caressed, kissed, explored, discovering what they already knew and rejoicing in the changes time had brought.

When they could bear no more, they each called the name of the other. Ben entered Laurel's willing body, filling her with all that he was, then beginning the rocking rhythm that she matched in perfect synchronization.

It was ecstasy. It was heated tension coiling tighter and tighter within them, lifting them upward to the place they wished to go…together. Higher. Hotter. The cadence now pounding, earthy and urgent.

And then they were there a second apart, flung over the top of reality and reason to burst upon the splendor that awaited them.

"Ben!"

"Ah, my Laurel."

They clung tightly to each other, then drifted slowly back down. Ben kissed Laurel, then moved off her, tucking her close to his side. He once again sifted his fingers through her hair, watching it fall over her breasts as she nestled her head on his shoulder.

Time lost meaning and sleep began to creep over their senses.

"You are the only man," Laurel said, her lashes drifting down, "I have ever made love with. Ever. I don't know why I need you to know that, I just do."

"And you are the only woman I've ever made love with, Laurel," Ben said. "There has been no one else since you left Willow Valley. And now you're home."

"Just for now, Ben. I don't know where I'll be in the future."

"We're not talking about the future," he said. "There's only tonight in this private world of ours. Remember?"

Laurel opened her eyes and kissed the strong column of Ben's neck.

"I remember," she said.

"No regrets?"

"No," she said. How could there be? She loved him beyond measure, would always love him. "No."

"Good," he said. Oh, how he wanted to tell her how he felt, declare his love just as he'd done so many years before. But he couldn't, wouldn't do that because it would serve no purpose. "That's good."

"It's strange somehow, Ben," Laurel said, "to have made love in this house that was only a fantasy, a dream so long ago and now really exists. It's almost unworldly, difficult to grasp somehow and...oh, I can't explain it."

"I understand what you're saying. I almost didn't build it because it was supposed to have been ours, but you were gone, and now here you are in this house we talked about so much back then. You're really here."

"Just for tonight."

"The night this house became a home."

Laurel didn't speak as threatening tears closed her throat. Ben reached down and drew the sheet and blankets up over them.

And they slept.

Sunlight poured through the skylight, nudging Laurel from a deep sleep. She opened her eyes, then frowned in confusion as she realized she had no idea where she was. In the next instant the fogginess of sleep dissipated and she gasped as she sat bolt upright on the bed.

"Oh, no," she said as she looked at the clock on the nightstand and saw that it was almost eight o'clock.

Laurel flung back the blankets, left the bed and began to search frantically around the room for her scattered clothes.

"Whoa, slow down, Laurel," Ben said, appearing in the doorway.

She began to pull on her clothes as she glared at him, seeing that his hair was still damp from a shower and he was wearing a crisp, clean uniform.

"I'm late for work," she said, "and my mother probably thinks I'm dead in a ditch. I had no intention of sleeping through the night. Oh, this is terrible. Darn it, where are my shoes?"

"Laurel," Ben said, walking forward, "chill. I called your mother and said you'd be arriving at the café late. She said she'd already figured that out and not to worry about it. She sounded very chipper, wasn't a bit upset as far as I could tell."

"I don't believe this," Laurel said, sitting down on the edge of the bed to put on the discovered shoes. "I told her I was coming out here to talk to you but— So when I didn't show up again at home, she just assumed...and she's calm, cool and chipper?"

"Yep." Ben paused. "Want some breakfast?"

"No."

"You're not in a very good mood, Laurel. At least have a cup of coffee."

"Benjamin Skeeter," she said, jumping to her feet again, "you know darn well that somehow, somehow, word will get out that I spent the night with you."

"You think?" he said, smiling.

"I know," she said, nearly shrieking. "And you know it, too, darn it. Why aren't you upset?"

Ben shrugged. "What's the point? I've lived here my entire life and I know how things work. Everyone went nuts about what I said regarding you not cutting your hair. The gossipmongers have already made up their minds that something is finally happening between us after your being back for four months. Let them enjoy themselves."

"Whatever," Laurel said, sighing. "I have no one to blame but myself because I should have left right after we... Never mind. What's done is done."

"Don't diminish what we shared, Laurel," Ben said quietly. "It was too special, too beautiful. No regrets, remember?"

"You're right," she said, nodding. "People will get tired of watching us, speculating about what is going on after a while, I suppose. We just won't comment if they say anything. You and I know it was just one night, a stolen night."

Ben closed the distance between them.

"Why?" he said, looking directly into her eyes.

"Why what?"

"Why does it have to be just one night? The facts are clear. You don't know if you're staying in Willow Valley or moving on, so there's no point in looking toward any future together. Why not live in the present, one day at a time, one night at a time?"

"I'm...I'm not sure that's a good idea, Ben."

"Neither of us can get hurt, Laurel, because we're not kidding ourselves here. What we had ten years ago is over. We're not the same people, not even close. But who we are now? We enjoy each other's company. We're going to be in close contact, along with Dove, to be certain that Grandfather is all right. And you can't deny that we make sweet, sweet love together. You might pack up and leave next week for all I know, but in the meantime..."

"This is starting to sound rather tacky, Ben," she said, folding her arms beneath her breasts.

"No, it isn't. Not if we're on the same page, understand that we're not making any long-term commitment. Think about it. I'll respect your decision." Ben paused. "I have to get going. I'm picking up

Bethany and going back over to Prescott for Yazzie's hearing in front of the judge. Have something to eat before you leave if you want to."

"No. No, I have to get home, shower and change, do something with this tangled mess that's supposed to be my hair and…"

"Hey," he said, drawing one thumb over her cheek. "Don't be sorry about last night. Please, Laurel, don't do that. It was ours, it was fantastic. Whether or not we're together again is up to you, but don't spoil what we shared. Please."

Laurel drew a shuddering breath. "You're right. It was wonderful. And ours. I'm not sorry it happened, Ben. I promise."

Ben nodded, brushed his lips over hers then turned and strode from the room. A few minutes later Laurel heard the front door close behind him and she sank down on the edge of the bed, her trembling legs refusing to hold her for another second. Two tears slid down her cheeks.

"Oh, God, Ben," she said, a sob catching in her throat. "I'm not sorry about last night because I love you so much. So very, very much."

She dashed the tears from her cheeks and stared up at the skylight.

Could she do what Ben had proposed? she thought. Could she continue to be with him even though they had no future together? Take one day, one night at a time, not think about the tomorrows of loneliness when she finally healed from the pain of what had happened in Virginia and moved on? Could she honestly do that?

She didn't know. She just didn't know.

As Ben drove away from the house to pick up Bethany on the reservation, he shook his head.

He was nuts, certifiably insane, he thought. He'd actually said it, opened his big mouth and told Laurel they should continue to be lovers for as long as it lasted. No strings attached. He hadn't even realized he was going to suggest such a thing until the words were out there, hanging in the air.

But the mere image in his mind of Laurel walking out of that house—that home—never to return had suddenly been more than he could bear. He had, he supposed, sounded very casual and "hey, why not?" about it, when within him he was frantic, wanted to beg Laurel to promise that she'd be with him again and...

God, he was losing it. He was so much in love with a woman who no longer loved him, didn't even trust him enough to tell him the secrets that were haunting her regarding why she'd come running back to Willow Valley. He was so pathetic it was a crime.

But he didn't care how lame he was. He would hope and pray that Laurel would agree to be with him for as long as it lasted, until she left him again. Then he'd relive the precious memories of their time together as he went through his days—and nights—alone.

But what if Laurel came to love him again as she once had? What if they could piece together their shattered dreams and have everything they'd planned to have so many years before? What if— No, he was kidding himself.

Laurel didn't trust him with her innermost secrets, and she sure as hell wasn't in love with him anymore, would never love him again.

So he'd swallow his stubborn Navajo pride and hope she'd agree to continue to be with him for as long as it lasted.

At least Laurel wouldn't know that he still loved her. At least she wouldn't know that she still possessed his heart, the very essence of his soul, and would for all time.

At least she wouldn't know that.

Chapter Eight

Laurel stood outside the rear door of the Windsong Café and fixed what she hoped was a somewhat pleasant yet rather nondescript expression on her face.

During the drive home from Ben's, through her shower, the braiding of her hair and donning fresh clothes, she'd lectured herself firmly regarding the necessity of presenting a relaxed, I-don't-have-a-care-in-the-world demeanor to the customers at the café.

Rumors and gossip regarding her, Ben and the previous night would build in intensity soon enough without her adding fuel to that annoying fire by appearing nervous, edgy and guilty as sin.

She entered the café, hung her jacket in the office then zoomed into the kitchen.

"Good morning, everyone," she sang out.

"Hello, sweetheart," Jane said, glancing over at Laurel from where she was frying eggs and bacon on the grill. "Things are a bit slow this morning, which is normal for the middle of the week. Dove is out front, though, having a cup of tea and a muffin."

"Oh, well, I guess I'll go talk to her and see how Eagle is today," Laurel said, picking up a pad and pencil. "Anything else I should know?"

"People are talking about Yazzie, of course," Jane said, sliding eggs onto a plate, "and how they hope the judge over in Prescott won't be too harsh in regard to what he did." Bacon joined the eggs. "Everyone is very proud of Eagle and how he tried to save his cousin from making such a dreadful mistake."

"Dove must be ready to burst her buttons with pride," Laurel said, nodding. "Is that the extent of…the buzz this morning?"

"No, not really," Jane said, adding hash browns and toast to the plate.

"No?" Laurel said weakly.

"There's a concern over the fact that we lost the

majority of the autumn leaves and what that will do to the tourist trade. All the shop owners are worried about the loss of revenue, including me." She turned and extended the plate toward Laurel. "Here. Give this to Cadillac, will you, please?"

"Sure," Laurel said, taking the plate. "There is nothing else being discussed out front?"

Jane shrugged. "Not that I know of. Go. Before that food gets cold."

Laurel frowned and left the kitchen, placing the plate in front of Cadillac moments later.

"So, Cadillac," she said, "what's new?"

"Waitin' to hear how Yazzie does in Prescott," Cadillac said. "Coffee?"

"Here you go," Laurel said, filling his mug. "What else is going on?"

"I'm done talking 'cause I'm eating my breakfast," Cadillac said, hunching over his plate.

"Enjoy," Laurel said, staring at him for a long moment to see if he'd speak further. "So much for that."

She came around the counter and crossed the floor to slide into the booth opposite Dove.

"Hi, Dove," she said. "How's Eagle?"

"He went to school looking like a raccoon with his black eyes," Dove said, then took a sip of tea. "He's quite the hero, you know. But we're so worried about Yazzie." She shook her head. "Not only that, I brought some blankets in this morning, and none of my regulars would take them because they're waiting to see what kind of tourist traffic we get over the weekend. Word will have reached Phoenix and beyond that the pretty leaves are about gone."

"And it's a long time before there's enough snow to bring the skiers," Laurel said.

Dove nodded and took a bite of muffin.

"I guess the topics of Yazzie and the rather frightening financial situation in town are the only things on people's minds today."

"Mmm," Dove said, nodding.

Laurel leaned forward. "You haven't heard about anything…else, Dove?"

"No one seems to have any information about Grandfather's health," Dove said. "I think we're going to have to confront him on the subject."

"Oh." Laurel glanced around. "It's pretty quiet in here. Maybe I should see if someone needs more coffee or whatever."

"Susie just did that," Dove said. "I saw her go table to table."

"Oh."

"Isn't it amazing how Ben's house turned out exactly the way he used to talk about how it would be?" Dove said. "He did most of the work himself, you know. It took him such a long time, but it was worth it. He gave me a tour when it was finished. I think the skylight in his bedroom is a marvelous touch, don't you?"

Laurel's eyes widened. "I beg your pardon?"

"Oh, Laurel," Dove said, laughing. "You should see the expression on your face. I could count on one hand the number of people who don't know you spent the night at Ben Skeeter's."

"But no one is gossiping about it?" Laurel said. "No one is giving me smug little smiles and... What is going on here?"

"Laurel," Dove said, reaching over and patting her hand, "people waited four months for this to happen and it finally did. They're satisfied because they feel things are now as they should be. End of story."

"But that's not how it is, Dove," Laurel said, her voice hushed so no one else could hear. "What I mean is... Oh, it's so complicated, confusing and...I just...I don't know what to do."

"Seems to me," Dove said, smiling, "that you already did it."

"Don't get cute," Laurel said, narrowing her eyes.

"There will be no more gossip or speculation about you and Ben, Laurel," Dove said. "Your privacy will now be respected." She paused. "The fact that you seem rather upset says there are things you and Ben need to address and work through. I'll listen if you want to talk, but I certainly won't press you about it. No one will."

Laurel nodded, then produced a small smile. "Being all grown up is a bummer sometimes, isn't it?"

"It certainly is," Dove said. "I've got to worry about how to feed a hungry Eagle if the economy of Willow Valley comes to a screeching halt because of that storm that went through." She sighed. "Everyone is so tired of not knowing how things will go from year to year, depending on the weather. It's such a helpless feeling, but I don't see it ever changing."

"I guess I've been gone so long I've forgotten how grim it can be," Laurel said. "I'm sorry, Dove. I was thinking only of myself again."

"Don't be so hard on yourself, Laurel," Dove said. "I know that what happened between you and Ben last night was very important to you both and no doubt raised a great many questions. But you two have to look to your hearts for the answers. No one can do it for you."

"You're so wise," Laurel said. "It's obvious that you're related to Grandfather." She paused. "As soon as things are settled about Yazzie and Ben has some time I guess the three of us should go visit Grandfather and find out what is really going on with him."

"Yes, we should." Dove reached for her purse.

"Well, I might as well go home and take my blankets with me. Word will spread through the rez about what happened over in Prescott. Yazzie's whole future depends on what takes place today."

"People's lives can change so quickly, can't they?" Laurel said. "It's unsettling, frightening, when you really dwell on it."

"Which is why," Dove said, scooting out of the booth, "it's better to dwell on hope and faith and believe that what is meant to be will be. I'll see you soon."

"Bye, Dove. Hug Eagle for me."

After Dove had left the café, Laurel stared out the window into the distance, seeing the nearly bare branches of the trees in every direction. As she watched, more leaves fell, skittered through the air and disappeared.

Dreams can be whisked away, Laurel thought, never to return, just like the autumn leaves. Someone could chase them, try to recapture them, hold fast and never again let them go, but that was impossible. Wasn't it?

The remainder of the morning and all through the afternoon time dragged slowly by as everyone from Willow Valley and the reservation waited for word of Yazzie's fate.

Laurel and her mother stayed at the café during the lull between the end of the lunch patrons and the dinner crowd rather than going home, so as not to miss any news of what had taken place in Prescott.

Just before six o'clock that evening Cadillac came bursting through the door of the restaurant. There were no tourists in the café at that moment, so Cadillac stood near the far end of the counter to share what he knew with everyone present.

"Sheriff Skeeter fixed things real fine for Yazzie," Cadillac said, obviously enjoying being in the spotlight. "Yep, just fine. Now you see, Yazzie didn't have a clue how to sell that stuff he took from the summer houses, so he stashed it in a cave in the mountains at the far side of the rez and covered it all with tarps.

"So Ben Skeeter told the judge that everything would be returned to who it belonged to. Then he did a big talking thing about how Yazzie had never been in trouble before and just messed up this one time...or something like that there and how he, that's the sheriff, you understand, would be checking on Yazzie all the time and how Yazzie was a fine boy and on and on, saying father kind of things like Yazzie was his very own son.

"Anyway, that judge person gave Yazzie a good scolding and said he'd better not get in any more trouble and how lucky he was to be having a sheriff in his corner and a mama who loved him and all.

"The judge told Yazzie to return that junk he took

and do one hundred hours of community service divided between town here and the rez. The judge said to wait until Yazzie had the cast off the arm Eagle busted for him so that Yazzie's community service would be sweatin' kind of work that would take two hands and a strong back.

"There you go," Cadillac said. "Yazzie is home with his mama, and Ben Skeeter did a fine job in Prescott in front of that judge. Now, don't go asking me a bunch of questions about the whole thing because I'm done talking for today and tomorrow put together. Sheriff Skeeter is headin' over this way to have him some dinner, so you can pester the daylights out of him if you want to."

Cadillac then placed one arm across his stomach and the other along his back and actually bowed to his audience before turning and hurrying out the door. A cheer went up from everyone there, smiles and slaps on the backs exchanged, and Laurel rushed to hug her mother.

"Yazzie is going to be all right," Laurel said. "Oh, thank God."

"And Ben Skeeter," Jane said, smiling. "Sounds like he did far more than the attorney assigned to Yazzie. Bethany must be so relieved. And I hope Yazzie understands how close he came to destroying his future. Oh, what foolish choices we all make at times." She paused. "Don't write Ben up a ticket when he comes for his dinner. That meal is compliments of the Windsong Café."

Laurel nodded and smiled just as another cheer went up accompanied by applause as Ben entered the building. He hesitated a moment, surprised at the reaction he had caused, then shook his head slightly.

"Cadillac," he said, "was here already." He nodded to those present, then slid into the first booth, setting his Stetson next to him on the bench with a weary sigh.

Laurel hurried over to stand next to him.

"Oh, Ben," she said, her eyes sparkling. "You did so much for Yazzie today. From what Cadillac told us, you were wonderful."

Ben chuckled. "Whatever. It worked, and that's what matters. I'm going to be the one to keep track of Yazzie's community service hours and make the assignments as to what he's to do after his arm heals."

"Cadillac said you sounded like a father when you were speaking of Yazzie," Laurel said. "I can believe that. You'd be a fabulous father."

"Well, at the moment I'm just a starving man," Ben said, dragging both hands down his face. "Whew. This has been one very long day. I was so afraid the judge would sentence Yazzie to some time in the detention center over there, but everything is going to be fine. Thanks to Eagle. And thanks to you knowing how to get through to Eagle."

"This happy ending has nothing to do with me," Laurel said. "How does beef stew, salad, corn bread and cherry pie sound? My mother says it's compliments of the Windsong Café for what you did today."

"That's very nice of her, and the menu you clicked off will be perfect. Bring it on."

The promised meal was soon set in front of Ben, who inhaled the delicious aromas.

"Can you sit?" he said to Laurel.

She glanced around the café, seeing that everything was under control, then settled opposite Ben in the booth. He started to eat the steaming-hot food.

"Mmm," he said.

"Should I call Dove with the news about Yazzie?" Laurel said. "Or do you think she and Eagle have heard by now?"

"I stopped by their place after dropping off Yazzie and Bethany," Ben said between bites. "Eagle smiled like a little kid on Christmas morning." He paused. "It took a lot of courage for Eagle to go after Yazzie last night and confront him like he did. Eagle really is a very mature young man."

"Dove raised him and the twins well," Laurel said, "when she was hardly more than a child herself."

"Yeah, but it wore her out," Ben said. "She says her days of being a mother are over when Eagle joins the Army in the spring."

"She told me that, too," Laurel said, folding her hands loosely on top of the table. "I think that's very sad. But then again, Dove isn't in love with anyone at the moment, so she could change her mind about the subject in the future. She might meet someone, fall in love and want to have her soul mate's baby. Could happen."

"Or not," Ben said. "She sure sounded adamant about it when we were chatting about kids one day last year. I was saying I'd always wanted a houseful and she was saying she'd already raised her houseful and that was that. I do believe I'm ready for that pie you spoke of, Ms. Laurel."

"Coming right up, Sheriff Skeeter," she said, smiling as she scooted out of the booth.

As recently as last year, she mused as she cut Ben a huge slice of pie, Ben had told Dove that he would like to have a bunch of kids. He'd always felt that way, ever since they were young and making plans for their future together. Ben would be such a caring, totally involved father. He would even change diapers and… Oh, stop. This sort of thinking was foolish, served no sensible purpose whatsoever.

When Laurel returned to Ben's table with the pie, she saw that a couple had taken her seat and were chattering away about Ben helping Yazzie. She placed the dessert in front of Ben, came back again to refill his coffee cup, then wandered away, ending up behind the counter, wiping off what was already clean.

"Ben is the hero of the moment," Jane said, appearing at Laurel's side. "He doesn't look too comfortable about all the attention he's getting."

"No, he isn't," Laurel said. "But he's very patient about it because he understands why it's happening and knows it will be old news when something else takes its place."

"I learned a great deal about Navajo patience from your father," Jane said. "About quiet acceptance of how things are and about what can be changed and what can't."

Laurel frowned. "Am I supposed to be getting a message here?"

"Oh, I don't know," Jane said, raising her eyebrows. "Are you? Think about it."

"Mother…"

"I have work to do in the kitchen," Jane said and walked away, leaving her daughter glaring at her back.

As soon as Ben finished his pie and coffee, he was on his feet, ready to escape from the attention he was receiving.

Outta here, he thought, settling his Stetson on his head. Enough was enough. He'd head for home, put his feet up and relax. Alone.

He looked over to the counter where Laurel was chatting with one of the shop owners.

Last night, he thought, had been fantastic, beyond words to describe it. The problem was that because it had taken place, it emphasized that tonight he was going home to an empty house and would sleep alone in his big bed. Laurel wouldn't be there. Damn.

Ben went down the hallway a bit and poked his head into the kitchen.

"Thanks for the delicious dinner, Jane," he said. "It was great and I appreciate it."

"You deserved it after what you did for Yazzie and Bethany," she said, crossing the large room to stand in front of him. "Everyone is grateful, Ben."

"Yeah, well, it's just an emotional bandage for Yazzie. He'll make amends for what he did, but it won't solve the real problem. He wants off the rez and away from here, and there's no easy answer as to how he can do that."

"What about the Army?" Jane said. "Like Eagle?"

"Yazzie sees that as just another bunch of people waiting to tell him what to do," Ben said, frowning. "He doesn't want any part of it. It's no wonder there's such a problem with alcohol abuse on the rez. There are so many who feel trapped out there with no way to improve their lives or... Whoa. Listen to me. I'm really getting on my soapbox here. I'm going home and shutting up."

"Do you know what's sad, Ben?" Jane said, wrapping her hands around her elbows. "Jimmy used to go on and on, saying very much what you just did. And here we are all these years later and the problem is still there. No answers have been found."

Ben smiled. "Well, that's depressing as hell."

"Isn't it, though?" Jane said, matching his smile.

"Somebody will figure out a solution, someday," Ben said. "I hope. Thanks again for the fine meal."

"You bet."

Ben walked back to the front of the café just as Laurel came around the counter.

"Good night, Laurel," he said, touching his fingertips to the brim of his Stetson. "Is everything still all right with you?" About last night? "You know what I mean?"

About last night? Laurel thought.

"Oh, yes, I'm fine," she said, smiling. "Thank you for asking."

"Did you think about what I said about—" Ben glanced around and lowered his voice "—living in the present and continuing to see each other? Did you, Laurel? Think about it?"

"I need more time to…to think about it."

"Sure," Ben said, nodding. "The last thing I want to do is pressure you. Well, I'm going home now. See ya."

"See ya."

Neither moved or hardly breathed as they looked directly into each other's eyes. Hearts began to beat in rapid tempos and heat coursed through their bodies like a rushing river out of control. Memories of the lovemaking they'd shared the previous night flitted enticingly in their mental visions. A pulse beat wildly in Ben's temple, and Laurel's lips parted slightly.

"Beggin' your pardon there, Sheriff Skeeter," Billy said, causing both Ben and Laurel to jerk at the sudden noise, "but could you get on with the kissing thing so I can pay my check, 'cause right now Miss Laurel she don't even know I'm standing here shuffling from one foot to the other. 'Kay?"

"Oh, dear heaven," Laurel said, dropping her face into her hands.

"You're absolutely right, Billy," Ben said, shoving his Stetson up with his thumb.

"He is?" Laurel said, raising her head to stare at Ben with wide eyes.

"Oh, yes, Miss Laurel," Ben said. "He is. Let it not be said that Sheriff Benjamin Skeeter compromised the fine, fine reputation of the Windsong Café.

The customer comes first, mustn't be kept waiting. Thank you for pointing that out, Billy."

"Well, sure thing," Billy said, appearing extremely pleased with himself. "Glad to help."

"Therefore," Ben said, framing Laurel's face in his hands.

"But…" Laurel said.

"Shh," Ben said.

Ben captured her lips in a searing kiss, then stepped back and tugged his Stetson low on his forehead. He spun around and headed for the door as Laurel stared after him in shock, her face flushed a pretty pink.

She attempted to ignore the fact that Ben Skeeter left the Windsong Café to the sound of cheers and applause, just as he'd received when he'd entered.

Chapter Nine

Laurel was not scheduled to work at the café the next day, so she spent the morning giving the house a thorough cleaning. She then prepared a casserole that would be ready to pop in the oven when her mother arrived home later, deciding Jane might like a chance to be waited on rather than having to cook.

She had just finished a lunch of a sandwich and a cup of soup when the telephone rang.

"Hello?" she said into the receiver of the wall phone in the kitchen.

"It's Ben. I called the café and your mother said

you weren't working today. Listen, Dove is here at the station. Are you free to come over?"

"Yes, but what's wrong?" Laurel said, her grip on the receiver tightening.

"We need to talk about Grandfather, Laurel," Ben said. "Now."

"Oh," Laurel said, pressing one hand to her forehead. "Oh, dear. I'm on my way, Ben."

When Laurel rushed into Ben's office at the station, Dove was sitting in one of the chairs opposite the desk with a tissue pressed to her nose. She had obviously been crying.

Ben was in his chair behind his desk, a deep frown on his face.

"Dove?" Laurel pulled the other chair close to Dove's. "What is it? What's happened to Grandfather?" She looked at Ben. "Ben, what is going on?"

Ben sighed and leaned forward, folding his arms on top of the desk.

"Dove went by to check on Grandfather," he said, "and there was smoke coming out of the pipe at the top of the center of Grandfather's hogan."

"His...hogan?" Laurel said, feeling the color drain from her face. "He left his trailer and moved into his hogan?"

"Yes," Dove said, then sniffled. "I was so upset

when I saw the smoke I didn't stay and attempt to talk to him. I just drove straight here. Oh, God, Laurel, you know what this means. We all do."

Laurel nodded as she struggled against threatening tears.

"Grandfather...Grandfather," Dove said, a sob catching in her throat, "is dying. He moved out of his trailer because he knows that there are so many Navajos on the rez that won't enter, let alone live in, a place where someone has died because they're frightened of the *chendi*."

"The evil spirit from the dead," Laurel said softly. "Grandfather is making certain that someone will be able to make a home in his trailer after he... I don't want to believe that he's..." She shook her head.

"I think that the three of us should go out there and talk to him," Ben said.

"Yes, of course, you're right," Dove said, getting to her feet.

"I'll have to take my handheld in case I'm needed for something," Ben said, rising. "You might as well drive your truck, Dove, so you won't have to come back into town to get it. So we'll go in three vehicles. We're going to look like a posse descending on Grandfather."

"Whatever it takes," Dove said, starting toward the door.

"Wait," Laurel said, pushing herself to her feet. "Shouldn't we talk this over, decide how we're going to approach Grandfather, what we're going to say?"

"His message is very clear, Laurel," Ben said, settling his Stetson on his head. "What we want are the details of what is wrong with him. Now we know why he was seen heading toward Phoenix."

"He went to keep an appointment with a doctor down there," Dove said.

"That's my guess," Ben said, nodding. "Let's go."

"But—" Laurel said.

"Laurel," Ben said, "why are you hesitating, attempting to postpone going out there? We have to talk to him."

"But ganging up on him isn't very respectful," she said, a frantic edge to her voice. "Maybe just Dove should go because she's his great-granddaughter. Family."

"We need you there, Laurel," Dove said, her voice rising. "You're a trained psychologist. You might hear something that is significant, and it could go right by me and Ben. Look how you understood what Eagle was doing in regard to Yazzie. What's wrong with you? Don't you want to try to help Grandfather?"

"Of course I do, Dove," Laurel said. "It's just that I…" She glanced at Ben, who was studying her intensely. "But don't count on me to be able to… Oh, never mind. Okay, okay, let's go out there."

Ben collected the handheld and the trio left the office. Without speaking further, they got into their vehicles and began the procession to the reservation.

Grandfather's circular hogan was about a hundred yards beyond his trailer. It was a fairly good size and had been constructed many years before out of sweetgrass that still held a lingering aroma of vanilla and hard-packed mud.

A rusted metal pipe was visible from the center of the top where smoke from a fire within was visible. A fire in a hogan was believed to be the Great Spirit of the Dinet, the People, believers in the old ways of the Navajos.

Like all Navajo hogans, the opening faced east to enable the occupant to see the rising sun. The floor of a hogan was hardened mud and straw and was often covered by hand-woven rugs. As was acceptable, Grandfather had replaced a blanket with a wooden door to keep out some of the cold during the long winters.

Laurel, Dove and Ben parked next to each other by Grandfather's trailer and met in front of the vehicles, staring at the hogan in the distance. Ben swept his gaze over the trailer.

"The windows are covered in boards," he said quietly. "And the cinder blocks he used for steps have been moved away from the entrance. Grandfather no longer lives in the trailer, nor does he intend to return to it."

"Dear heaven," Laurel whispered.

Dove closed her eyes. "I won't cry. I won't cry. I won't cry." She opened her eyes again and drew a steadying breath. "Oh, I hope I don't cry."

They walked to within twenty feet of the door to the hogan and stopped, as was Navajo custom.

"*Ya at eeh,* Grandfather," Ben called in greeting. "It's Ben, Laurel and Dove. We are asking permission to enter your hogan."

Seconds ticked slowly by.

"He's not going to acknowledge us," Laurel said quietly.

"Be patient," Ben said.

A full minute passed in agonizing silence. Then the wooden door was pushed outward, although Grandfather did not appear in the doorway.

"Okay," Ben said, starting forward. "Here we go."

Ben and Dove went three feet, then realized that Laurel hadn't moved. They turned to look back at her.

"Laurel?" Dove said. "Are you coming?"

"I…" Laurel wrapped her hands around her elbows as a shiver coursed through her. "Yes."

The three entered the hogan, which was large enough for even Ben to stand erect, and he pulled the door closed behind him.

Grandfather was sitting cross-legged on a rug in front of a fire burning in a shallow pit in the center of the hogan, and his hands were resting on his knees as he stared into the flames.

His silver hair was in two long braids hanging down his back, and he was wearing well-worn jeans, a long-sleeved faded flannel shirt and moccasins. His face was tanned and wrinkled beyond his heritage from years of being in the sun and wind.

Around his neck on a rawhide thong strung with red, white and blue beads was the bronze code-talker medallion that fell to the center of his chest.

"May we sit down, Grandfather?" Ben said.

Grandfather nodded.

The trio settled on a rug across from Grandfather, crossing their legs just as he was. Laurel and Dove sat on either side of Ben. The fire burned between them and Grandfather, causing them to look at him through the rising pale gray smoke. They slipped off their coats and allowed them to fall to the ground behind them. Dove opened her mouth to speak, but Ben reached over and touched her arm, shaking his head.

They waited.

"When you were children," Grandfather said

finally, still staring into the fire, "I smiled as I watched you play together outside my home. You were happy. Your laughter was carried by the wind and you brought me great joy.

"Benjamin was *Moasi,* the cat, moving with ease in his body, comfortable even then with his manhood.

"Dove was *Naastsosi,* the mouse, so timid at times, afraid to take risks, often backing away from a new game that was frightening to her.

"Laurel was *Dahetihhi,* the hummingbird. So curious, flitting here, then there and farther, wishing to see all that life offered. Appearing very fragile yet having great strengths.

"Do you remember those names of your child-hood?"

"Yes," Ben and Dove said in unison as Laurel nodded.

"Good, that is good," Grandfather said. "Those names still belong to you, as they are true to who you are now, as well as then."

Grandfather stopped speaking and another heavy silence fell.

"I have seen," he said, after several long minutes, "the *neasjah.*"

"No," Dove said, fresh tears filling her eyes. "No, Grandfather, not the owl. Please don't say...don't say you saw the owl."

"There is no reason to feel sorrow, Dove," Grandfather said. "*Neasjah* doesn't alarm me. The message is clear and I'm prepared for what is to come. That's why I have moved into my hogan. So someone will be able to make a home of my trailer when I am gone."

Dove sniffled and shook her head.

"What ails you, Grandfather?" Ben said quietly.

"The Navajos of old called it the wasting disease," he said. "Now it is known as cancer."

"Can't the doctors do something?" Ben said. "Surgery? Treatments of chemotherapy and radiation?"

Grandfather nodded. "They wish to do those things, but I chose not to. I have pills for pain when it comes. No, I won't have surgery or the harsh treatments they explained to me."

"Why not?" Ben said. "Cancer isn't an automatic death sentence. What the doctors are proposing might save your life or at least give you more time to…"

"*Dooda.* No." Grandfather covered the code-talker medallion with one hand. "You must understand. I wish to die with dignity here on the land that I love, not in a cold, sterile hospital surrounded by strangers.

"I am satisfied, at peace with my life, with what I have done. I don't fear crossing the rainbow bridge that will take me from the human world to the other side and the life beyond." He paused. "I wish to be alone now. I'm tired. Thank you for your visit."

"But…" Dove said.

"Not now, Dove," Ben said, rising in a fluid motion. "It's time for us to go. *Hagoonee*, Grandfather. Goodbye for now. We'll see you again soon."

Grandfather nodded and closed his eyes.

The three gathered their coats, then Ben led Dove from the hogan with Laurel following slowly behind. They walked in silence back to where they had parked their vehicles. Ben stepped in front of Laurel, his dark eyes flashing with anger.

"You didn't say one damn word while we were in that hogan, Laurel," he said, his voice rough. "Nothing. It was obvious back in town that you didn't even want to come out here. What's the matter with you?"

He pointed toward the hogan. "That's Grandfather in there, Laurel. Our beloved Grandfather. You're a psychologist, for God's sake. You were taught how to reach people, like someone who initially refuses medical treatment for whatever they've been diagnosed with. Right? Damn straight.

"But did you even attempt to reason with Grandfather? No. You just sat there like it was no big deal, as though you were bored out of your mind."

Ben spun around, strode three paces away then

turned and came back to tower over Laurel, who pressed her lips tightly together and refused to meet his angry gaze.

"Why didn't I see this in you?" he said, his voice raspy. "You are so cold, so self-centered, so unfeeling. Is this what you learned in Virginia, Laurel? To care only about yourself?"

"Ben, don't," Dove said, placing one hand on his arm. "You're going to say things in the heat of the moment that you'll regret later."

Ben shook off Dove's hand. "I'm saying what needs to be said. I want answers, Laurel. Why are you refusing to talk to Grandfather, to use your knowledge, your training? Why? Why in the hell did you come back to Willow Valley if none of us mean anything to you now? How can you turn your back on our Grandfather?"

Laurel covered her ears with her hands. "Leave me alone. You don't understand why I can't try to convince Grandfather to… You just don't understand. And it's none of your business why I came home to Willow Valley. Just leave me alone, Ben Skeeter. Don't speak to me, don't come near me. Not ever again. Not ever."

Laurel ran to her van and minutes later drove away, leaving a cloud of dust behind her.

"Damn it," Ben said, then made a fist and punched the side of his vehicle.

"Ben, stop it," Dove said. "I've never seen you act this way in all the years I've known you. Laurel didn't deserve what you just did to her, the hateful things you said. You're upset because Grandfather is going to die and has made his decision as to how he wishes to leave us. We're all devastated about it, including Laurel.

"You're frustrated, feel helpless, because you know that nothing anyone says now will change Grandfather's mind and you took out those emotions on Laurel."

"She might have been able to reach him, get through to him," Ben said, a muscle ticking in his jaw. "She didn't even try, Dove. She didn't say one damn word to him in that hogan."

"There was nothing to say," Dove said, her eyes filling with fresh tears. "Grandfather wants to die with dignity here on the reservation and that is exactly what he will do. We all have to respect him and his wishes. We have to, Ben. Laurel knew that. I don't want to accept it, but I will and so will you." She shook her head. "You owe Laurel an apology for lashing out at her like you did. You were wrong, Ben. I hope she'll forgive you."

"*I* owe *her* an apology? Yeah, okay, maybe I was too rough on her just now, dumped how I was feeling on her, but what about how she just waltzed back into town and stirred up old memories and opened old wounds? How she refused to even explain why she's here, how long she's staying, what her plans are for the future? But *I* owe *her* an apology? Do you have any idea what it's done to me to have Laurel back in Willow Valley, Dove? Do you?"

"Yes," she said softly. "I do, because you're still in love with her, never stopped loving her during all the years she was gone. Did it ever occur to you how difficult it might be for her to have returned here? To see you, remember what you two had? Oh, never mind. You're in no mood to listen to reason. You're as stubborn as Grandfather."

"Why did she run home, Dove? Why did she leave Virginia like a...a frightened child, or whatever?"

"I don't know, Ben. She's not ready to talk about it yet."

"She won't tell you, but you still consider her your best friend?" he said, raising his eyebrows. "Don't you get it? Her friendship, her love, is all done on her terms with no regard for other people's feelings."

"I don't believe that," Dove said. "True friendship, true love, is patient. You're the one who doesn't get it, Ben. You want answers from Laurel now. You want Grandfather to undergo treatment for his cancer. You want, you want, you want. You'd feel better if people would do things your way, so why don't they just shut up and do it? You'd better take a long look at yourself, Benjamin Skeeter, and get your head on straight."

Ben stared up at the sky for a long moment, then looked at Dove again.

"Everything is a mess, just totally screwed up," he said. "My mind is like a jumbled maze and nothing makes sense right now."

"Would you like to get out of the cold and come to my house for some tea? We could talk about all of this."

"No," Ben said. "Thanks, but I'm going to have to work through all this on my own. Besides, I have to get back to town and see Doc Willie."

"Doc Willie?" Dove said, frowning. "Why?"

"Because when I pitched my fit," he said, grimacing, "threw my less-than-mature tantrum and clobbered my vehicle, I broke my damn hand."

The next day was Friday. Then Saturday arrived, and by noon everyone in Willow Valley realized that their fears had come true. The tourists had heard that the autumn leaves were no longer on the trees to be enjoyed as a glorious, beautiful gift from nature. They would not return to Willow Valley until the snow came and enough had fallen to make it possible to ski.

Word had also spread about Grandfather's illness and his decision to live out his remaining days in the hogan. Gifts of food, beads, feathers, blankets and baskets were left outside the wooden door of the hogan, but no one disturbed him by asking to come inside. They watched for the smoke to continue to rise from the center of the hogan as a sign that Grandfather was still with them.

A dozen different stories circulated as to how Sheriff Skeeter broke his right hand; some tales were outrageous, but Ben Skeeter had nothing to say on the subject.

A state of gloom settled over the town and the reservation. People were saddened by the news of Grandfather as well as worried beyond measure about the lack of revenue that the shortened fall tourist season meant.

Laurel told her mother that it wasn't fair for Laurel to work at the Windsong Café and take hours from the regular employees when there were only the locals eating there. Jane reluctantly agreed that there wasn't money enough to pay Laurel when she really wasn't needed on the staff.

Laurel spent hours in her bedroom, reliving the scene with Ben outside Grandfather's hogan, unable to quiet the sound of Ben's angry words that beat against her mind over and over again. On Sunday evening she told her mother what Ben had accused her of after they'd seen Grandfather.

"I didn't intend to burden you with this," Laurel said, sitting on one end of the sofa while her mother sat on the other. "It's just that I'm driving myself crazy, hearing Ben's words slamming against my brain and…" She shook her head.

"Oh, sweetheart," Jane said, "nothing you might have said to Grandfather would have changed his mind. We all have to respect his wishes. Ben will come to understand that in time."

"That's not the point," Laurel said, throwing up her hands. "I didn't say anything to Grandfather, not even that I understood and respected his choice. Mother, I froze. I was so terrified that I'd say the wrong thing to him that I couldn't speak. I couldn't. I didn't say how much I loved him, would miss him…nothing. Grandfather must think the same things of me that Ben does. That I'm self-centered, don't care—"

"That's enough," Jane interrupted. "We're talking about Grandfather, remember? He is the wisest man I have ever known." She smiled. "Even wiser than your father, I'll have you know. Grandfather has no doubts in his heart as to how you feel about him. Shame on you for thinking otherwise. Grandfather deserves better than that from you."

Laurel wrapped her hands around her elbows and nodded. "You're right. Yes, of course, you're right. But Ben...never mind."

"Ben needs to hear the truth of why you returned to Willow Valley, the truth of what happened in Virginia, Laurel. Your silence is becoming a high and dangerous wall between the two of you. You were reaching out to each other at long last, and now? Oh, yes, it's a very dangerous wall, indeed."

"I wish I could talk to Grandfather about Ben, about Virginia," Laurel said. "He was always there for me, especially after Dad died. But I can't bother him with my problems. Not now, with him being so ill."

"Oh, my darling girl, you are so wrong," Jane said. "Grandfather would be honored to feel that you still believe in his wisdom even though his body is failing him. Go to him. If he's in pain or too tired when you visit, he'll tell you to come another time. You know Grandfather is there for you. You believe that in your heart, Laurel. You do. I believe in *my* heart that he knows you are troubled and he's waiting for you."

"I... Oh, I don't know what to do."

"Think about it. At least promise me that you'll think about going to your Grandfather."

"Yes, I'll think about it."

"Good. That's something, at least, on my side of

the scorecard." Jane paused, then laughed softly. "Billy told me that he knows for a fact that Grandfather's horse bit Ben's hand and broke it."

"Thunder?" Laurel said, her eyes widening. "That's the silliest thing I've ever heard. That tops Cadillac saying that a ghost of a dead coyote darted in front of Ben and caused him to fall, breaking his hand. Dumb." She frowned. "I wonder why Ben just doesn't explain how it happened and stop all the ridiculous stories?"

"Because he's embarrassed," Jane said. "He was so upset outside of Grandfather's hogan after you three came out that he punched his vehicle."

"You're kidding."

"No. Dove told me what happened. She gave him a piece of her mind for speaking to you the way he did, told him he'd taken out his sorrow about Grandfather on you—oh, and on his SUV. Ben Skeeter is not about to confess to the world that he behaved like a naughty four-year-old and hit his vehicle."

"He's not about to change his mind about what he said to me, either." Laurel sighed. "Ben believes every word."

"You don't know that, Laurel."

"Yes, I do, because when I really look back on how I acted inside that hogan, I would come to the same conclusions about me, too. I don't blame Ben for the way he perceived my behavior that day. Self-centered and silent. Too wrapped up in me to reach out to our Grandfather."

"Then set Ben straight."

"It's time for the news, Mother. Would you turn on the television, please?"

Jane rolled her eyes in frustration, then reached for the remote.

Chapter Ten

The governing board of Willow Valley, which was made up of a mayor and city council, had not held an official meeting in nearly five years, due to the fact that there was really nothing for them to discuss.

The mayor was sixty-year-old Donald Smith, who was also the president of the chamber of commerce. Don owned and operated an antique store with Mary-ellen, his wife of forty years.

It had been decided many years before, when Don accepted the office of president, that it would appear more impressive on tourist information if there was a mayor and city council to list on the color brochure.

The city council was made up of five business owners, Jane having taken Jimmy Windsong's place after his death.

The meeting held five years previously had been to appoint one of the shop owners the job of changing the population figure once a year on the sign on the edge of town announcing that a person was now entering Willow Valley, Arizona.

On Monday morning Don sat on one of the stools at the counter at Windsong Café and drank a cup of coffee that accompanied a huge fresh-from-the-oven cinnamon roll. Don was short, round and balding. Every Christmas he dressed up as Santa Claus for the annual party held in the high-school multipurpose room for the children of Willow Valley and the reservation. Don was a cheerful man who had a smile always at the ready. But not today.

"Then you agree with me, Jane," Don said. "Willow Valley is in trouble because of losing the tourist trade so early this year."

"Oh, yes, Don, I certainly do agree with you," Jane said, filling his coffee cup. "I can't remember the autumn tourist season ever being this short. That storm that came up so fast and blew through here has had far-reaching ramifications."

Don nodded. "As mayor, per se, I feel as though I should do something. You know, call a meeting of the city council and brainstorm ideas about how we're all going to get through this. But for the life of me I can't think of one plan I could suggest that would be the least bit helpful to any one of us."

"Well, as a member of the city council, per se," Jane said, sighing, "neither can I. We're at the mercy of nature, Don, and nothing is going to change that. We'll all just have to get through this as best we can." She paused. "I do worry, though, that there will be people on the reservation who might go hungry, actually not have money for food because they were laid off or couldn't sell their handmade crafts in the shops."

Don nodded and took a bite of the warm roll. "Don't tell Maryellen I ate this thing. Doc Willie says I have to lose twenty-five pounds. Just because he's seventy years old and weighs the same as he did in high school he thinks everyone else should be skinny as a post. Anyway, this is comfort food. I'm worried about the people in our town and on the rez."

"So am I," Jane said, frowning.

Ben entered the café and slid onto the stool next to Don.

"Good morning, Ben," Jane said. "Coffee?"

"Please," he said, nodding. "How are you, Don?"

"Drowning my concerns in this cinnamon roll," Don said. "Between the economy here being rock-bottom low and the sad, sad news about Grandfather, it's as though there's a dark cloud hanging over everything, Ben."

"Yeah, I know what you mean," Ben said, managing to pick up the coffee cup with his right hand despite the cast Doc Willie had put on it.

"I heard," Don said, "that you broke your hand when you were arm wrestling with your deputy. Can't remember which fella it was, though, now that I think about it. It didn't make much sense, either, because you're bigger than all those guys on your staff."

Ben took another sip of the hot coffee. "That's not how I broke my hand, Don."

"Didn't think so," Don said. "Want to share the true story, Sheriff Skeeter?"

"Nope."

"Didn't think that would happen, either," Don said, popping the last bite of roll into his mouth. "Well, I'd best get back to the store. Jane, if you come up with a genius-level idea about what we can do to create some revenue around here, be sure and let me know."

"I certainly will," she said. "Say hello to Maryellen for me."

Don left the café, and Jane tended to coffee cups along the counter, then returned to stand in front of Ben.

"Laurel isn't working here for now," she said. "I just couldn't afford to pay her, and she agreed that it wasn't fair to our long-standing employees to be getting what would be their tips and what have you."

"Mmm," Ben said, staring into his cup.

"Laurel's keeping the house so clean it squeaks, and she has my dinner ready in the evening."

"Mmm."

"I think she'll be getting bored, though," Jane went on. "It's too bad she doesn't have a hobby, a craft she's good at, like Dove."

"Mmm," Ben said.

"Of course, in Dove's case, the things she makes put food on the table for her and Eagle, and the shops aren't taking Dove's work because there aren't enough tourists in town to buy things."

"Mmm," Ben said, then drained his cup.

"Well, gosh, Ben," Jane said, planting one hand on her hip. "Don't talk so much and not let me get a word in edgewise."

Ben met Jane's frowning gaze.

"Sorry," he said. "I just have a lot on my mind, I guess. Everyone I speak with is down in the dumps. They're worried about the lack of revenue and feel so helpless about Grandfather." He paused. "I'm also dealing with…" He cleared his throat. "Never mind."

Jane leaned over and lowered her voice.

"Dealing with the confrontation you had with Laurel after the visit to Grandfather's hogan? Did it ever occur to you that you two should talk that through, clear up the misunderstanding that it actually was?"

"It has come to light," Ben said, tugging his Stetson low on his forehead, "that Laurel and I have had a communication problem of very long standing. We just don't seem to be able to talk to each other very well."

"Well, la-di-da," Jane said. "So you figure, what's the point in attempting to get the facts straight? I guess you don't care enough to try to do that."

"That's not true," Ben said. "I…"

"You what?"

"I have to get back to work," Ben said, getting to his feet. He dropped a bill on the counter. "Thanks for the coffee."

"Mmm," Jane said, glowering at him.

Outside, Ben glanced around and shook his head as he saw the nearly empty sidewalks.

Things hadn't looked much better over the weekend, he thought, because people had no reason to come to Willow Valley. The situation was bad, very bad.

Drinking on the rez was going to increase, which would result in more domestic-violence calls coming into the office. People with money worries had a tendency to drown their problems in liquor, then take out their frustrations on those they loved. There had to be a solution to everyone being at the mercy of nature, but he sure as hell didn't know what the answer was.

Ben drove his patrol car slowly through town, then cruised through the residential section.

He was not, he told himself, going to turn onto the street where Laurel was living with Jane. But then again, it wasn't fair to the other homeowners to not check things out and... Aw, Skeeter, shut up. Who are you kidding?

As Ben approached the Windsong home, his eyes widened and he pressed on the brake in front of the house. He parked at the curb and moments later was striding across the small yard to where Laurel was standing high on a rickety wooden ladder she'd rested against the front of the house.

"What in the hell are you doing up there?" he yelled, halting by the side of the ladder.

"Aakk," Laurel screamed, gripping the gutter with both hands. She looked down at Ben. "Darn it, you scared me to death, Benjamin Skeeter."

"Answer the question," he said, none too quietly.

"I'm cleaning the wet leaves out of the gutters," she said, dropping a clump that landed just in front of him. "What does it look like I'm doing?"

"It looks like you're working up to a stay in the hospital when you fall off that ladder that was probably built during the Civil War," he said, volume still on high. "There are people in town who you can hire to do that stuff, Laurel."

"And they charge a fee," she said, flinging another handful of leaves in Ben's direction. "We're watching our pennies in this household, and because I'm not working at the café I decided to do this myself. Since it's not against the law, Sheriff, to clean out one's gutters, I suggest you go catch a crook and earn your keep."

"If you hit me with one soggy leaf, just one," he said, "I'm going to arrest you for assaulting an officer of the law and throw you in jail."

"Now that," Laurel said, tossing some leaves over her shoulder, "was funny."

"I'm not kidding, Laurel Windsong. Get down off that thing right now."

"No."

"Then I'll come up and get you."

"Don't you dare. This ladder can hardly hold me, let alone you, too. Are you going for a whole collection of casts on your body? By the way, did you dent your vehicle when you hit it?"

"Who told you that I…" Ben narrowed his eyes. "Dove."

"I haven't seen Dove."

"Well, she told someone who told someone else who told you," he said. "I know how these things go." Ben paused. "Laurel, please, be reasonable. That ladder is dangerous. Look, I'll bring my ladder over after I get off duty and clean those gutters."

"No, thank you."

"Fine," Ben said, raising both hands. "Then I'll stand here so I can call for the ambulance when the rungs on that piece of junk let go. How's that?"

"Suit yourself," she said, reaching farther along the gutter to scoop out more leaves.

As Laurel leaned far to the right, the ladder tilted, then the rung she was standing on snapped in the middle and she lost her footing. In the next second she was airborne, heading swiftly backward toward the ground, a scream escaping from her throat.

Ben took one long step, held out his arms and caught Laurel, who was wearing her red jacket that matched her van. With one arm beneath Laurel's knees and the other around her back, Ben staggered, then steadied.

Laurel was so stunned by the frightening fall that she didn't move, her eyes wide as saucers, her lips slightly parted.

"Laurel," Ben said, "breathe."

She jerked, drew in a huge, wobbly breath, then

went limp in Ben's arms. He shifted her closer to his chest and tightened his hold on her.

"Oh, my goodness," she said, turning her head slowly to look up at Ben. "That was so scary. Thank you, Ben. I am so grateful that you…"

Laurel totally forgot what she was going to say as she realized that Ben's lips were only inches from hers and that his dark eyes were radiating desire so intense it was causing heat to churn deep within her.

"I hope you didn't hurt your hand when you caught me," she said, hearing the strange squeaky sound that was her voice.

"No."

"You…you can put me down now."

"No."

"You were very angry with me, Ben, and then I told you to stay away from me, but here you are in my front yard, and that doesn't make sense."

"No." Ben lowered his head toward hers. "But this does."

Ben's lips melted over Laurel's, his tongue parting her lips and delving into the sweet darkness of her mouth. She shifted one arm to enable her to encircle his neck with her hand, pressing his mouth harder onto hers.

The kiss was heat that was fanned into licking flames of desire so hot it raged within them like a prairie fire out of control. Hearts raced, and their breathing became labored as the kiss intensified even more and went on and on.

"Yo, Sheriff Skeeter," a male voice yelled from a passing truck. "Way to go, man."

Ben's head snapped up. Laurel stiffened in his arms.

"Oh, good grief," she whispered, not having enough air left in her lungs to speak louder.

"Aw, hell," Ben said, then carefully lowered Laurel to her feet. "Okay? Are you steady? Over the shock of the fall?"

"Yes, I'm…I'm fine," she said, straightening her jacket so she could avert her gaze from Ben's. "Thank you again for…"

"Laurel, I'm sorry," Ben interrupted. "I was way out of line when I jumped your case after we saw Grandfather. No one is going to change his mind about the choice he's made, and I was upset, frustrated. But that's no excuse. Please forgive me for being such a jerk. Please?"

"Yes, of course," she said. "I should have said something to Grandfather, anything to let him know that I love him, respect what he's doing. I'm sorry, too, for the way I acted that day at the hogan. I plan to visit Grandfather and assure him that I understand his wishes."

"Laurel, look at me," Ben said, his voice gritty.

"Oh, I don't think that would be a very good idea right now."

"Look. At. Me."

Laurel raised her head slowly to meet Ben's gaze, her breath catching as she saw the desire still radiating in his eyes, knowing it was mirrored in her own.

"I know you told me to stay away from you," he said, "but I couldn't. I can't. I want to be with you, talk and laugh, give and get comfort over what is happening to Grandfather. I want...I want to make love with you for hours and hours and...

"Aw, damn it, Laurel, don't you get it? I'm still in love with you, never stopped loving you. There. I've said it out loud. I love you, Laurel Windsong. Always have, always will."

Laurel's eyes filled with sudden and unwelcome tears.

"I love you, too, Ben," she said, a sob escaping from her lips. "I don't have the emotional energy to deny it. But, Ben, we're not the same people we were ten years ago. We're not."

"You're Laurel," he said, his jaw tightening. "My Laurel. That's all I need to know."

"No, it isn't all you need to know," she said, tears spilling onto her cheeks as she took a step backward.

"Something happened in Virginia that…" She pressed shaking fingertips to her lips and shook her head.

Ben attempted to grip her shoulders, but his hand with the cast slipped off her jacket, and she took another step backward.

"Don't run from me," he said. "Talk to me. Tell me what happened to you in Virginia. We'll deal with it, Laurel. Together."

"No, no, no. It's something I have to do on my own. It changed everything for me. I don't know who I am or what I'm going to do with my life. Okay, yes, okay, I love you. But I can't be with you, pretend I'm the same person I was before, because I'm not. I'm just…not. I need time to…"

"Then I'll wait," Ben said, tugging his Stetson low on his forehead. "I've waited ten years, I can wait some more. The hell with my pride. Until you tell me that you no longer love me, that you're leaving me again, leaving Willow Valley and not coming back, I'll wait."

"I can't promise you anything," she said, more tears streaking her cheeks and running along her neck. "I'm searching desperately for inner peace and I don't know if I'll ever find it. *I just don't know.*"

Ben stared at her for a long, heart-stopping moment, closed the distance between them, then bent down and brushed his lips over hers.

"I'll wait, Laurel," he said, his voice hoarse with emotion.

Then he turned and strode across the yard, driving away minutes later without looking at her again. Laurel watched him go, her heart aching as she felt nearly crushed by the weight of a mixture of joy beyond measure that Ben still loved her, but unable to ignore the truth that she might never be for him what she wished to be, what he deserved to have.

"Oh, Grandfather," she said, crying openly. "I need your help so much, your wisdom. Please, Grandfather, help me."

The next morning, after a nearly sleepless night, Laurel drove to the reservation and was welcomed by Dove, who ushered Laurel into the kitchen, draped her red jacket on a chair and soon placed mugs of tea in front of both of them as they sat opposite at the old Formica table.

"You look terrible," Dove said.

"Thanks a bunch," Laurel said, producing a small smile that disappeared in the next instant. "Um...how's Eagle?"

"Fine."

"And Yazzie?" Laurel said.

"He's learned some very important lessons. I believe he's on the right road, now, I really do."

"Good," Laurel said, nodding. "That's good."

"Mmm," Dove said.

"Are you worried about finances because of the shortened tourist season, Dove?"

"Yes, I'm very concerned, as is everyone I talk to."

"Yeah," Laurel said, nodding. "The situation is bad, very frightening."

"Yes, it is." Dove paused. "Grandfather had Eagle and Yazzie take Thunder over to Molly Redhawk's place. She has a decent barn and those corrals we all helped build for her years ago. Thunder is going to live there, now. I think that's the last of his personal business that Grandfather has to tend to, Laurel."

"Oh, Dove, it's so hard to believe that Grandfather is going to leave us," Laurel said, shaking her head.

"Yes, it is."

"Dove, I was talking to my mother, saying how much I wished I could go to Grandfather with my problems as I've always done, but that I knew I couldn't do that because he's so ill. She said I was wrong, that Grandfather would be pleased to know that I still trust in his wisdom. What do you think?"

"I thoroughly agree with your mother," Dove said, nodding. "Grandfather would want you to come to him."

"I'd like to talk to him about Ben," Laurel said,

tracing the top edge of the mug with a fingertip. "Ben... Well, you see, he said he stills loves me. Then I told him that I still love him but because of what happened in Virginia I'm not who I was before. I'm such a confused mess."

Dove got to her feet, came around the table and snatched Laurel's jacket from the chair and shoved it at her.

"Goodbye, Laurel," Dove said. "Give Grandfather my love."

"But…"

"Goodbye," Dove said, folding her arms over her breasts.

"I believe," Laurel said, lifting her chin, "that I'll go visit Grandfather now."

"I'm glad to hear that," Dove said, smiling.

When Laurel stood outside Grandfather's hogan a short time later, having not yet called out a greeting announcing her arrival, she was in the process of convincing herself that perhaps another day would be best for this baring of her soul. She took one step backward, then her breath caught as the wooden door to the hogan opened and Grandfather appeared, leaning on a walking stick.

"Come in, *Dahetihhi*," he said. "Don't flit away like the hummingbird."

Laurel took a steadying breath and walked forward to stand in front of Grandfather.

"Are you well enough today to listen to my troubles?" she said.

"Yes, my Laurel Windsong. It's time for you to tell me of your *nanilin*. The secret you have kept since you arrived home. Enter now. It's cold out there."

Laurel smiled and went into the hogan. She removed her coat, then sat next to Grandfather on a blanket in front of the fire.

"It's peaceful in here," Laurel said quietly. "I just wish that your being in the hogan didn't mean... Oh, Grandfather, I'm going to miss you so much."

"Hush," Grandfather said gently. "Some things can't be changed, others can. We have to accept what is true." He paused. "Tell me, Laurel, are you afraid of the *chendi?* The evil spirit of the dead?"

"No. My father taught me not to fear the *chendi*."

"That is good," Grandfather said, nodding. "Jimmy Windsong was a wise man. After I leave Mother Earth, you might wish to come to this peaceful hogan before it is sealed for all time. There is much comfort to be found in this place."

"Thank you, Grandfather. I'll...I'll remember that."

"I want to show you something."

Grandfather reached into the breast pocket of the flannel shirt he wore and removed a deep blue turquoise stone. It was the size of a quarter and about a half inch high in the center.

"Oh, that's lovely," Laurel said. "That's my favorite shade of turquoise."

"My mother gave me this as I was leaving to go to the war, where I became a code-talker. I was so young, no more in years than Eagle and Yazzie," Grandfather said, closing his hand around the piece of turquoise. "My mother made it clear that the stone held no magical powers, had not been presented at a ceremony for that purpose."

Laurel nodded, her gaze riveted on Grandfather's face.

"She knew there would be times in that faraway place I was to go to when I would be frightened, confused, wishing to run away and return to my home. The purpose of the stone was to make me stop, touch it and, in that quiet moment, reach deep within myself for strength and courage I was forgetting I had. My fingers found the stone many, many times while I was away. I will hold it again in the days ahead as I face what is yet to come." He slipped the stone back into his pocket.

Laurel blinked away threatening tears.

"I am telling you this, Laurel Windsong, my little *Dahetihhi,* because you are frightened, confused, and you have run from your fears. You have not reached within you for the strength you have, that I know in my heart that you have. You must do this if you wish to be free of the ghosts that hold you fast."

"I don't know if I have the strength you speak of, Grandfather," Laurel said, tears echoing in her voice. "I just don't know."

"Tell me your story," he said. "It is time."

Ben drove the patrol car to the far edges of the reservation, looking for any sign of trouble but finding none.

He stopped at Molly Redhawk's and gave her some money toward Thunder's feed. Molly told him that the proud horse was feeling his many years and was beginning to show symptoms of failing health. Ben brushed the stallion until he gleamed, talking to him the entire time in a quiet, soothing voice.

On his way back he decided to drive by Grandfather's to be certain that smoke was still visible coming from the top of the hogan.

"Laurel," he said aloud as he saw the red van parked by the hogan.

This was good, Ben thought, his heart racing. Laurel was talking to Grandfather, seeking the great man's wisdom. Was she telling Grandfather of her love for him, and that he loved her? Was she revealing what had happened to her in Virginia? Oh, he hoped so. His future—their future together—could depend on what took place within that hogan.

Ben turned off the ignition to the patrol car and crossed his arms on top of the steering wheel, staring at the hogan, wishing he could hear what was being said inside.

He had to know, he thought frantically. He was now living hour to hour, waiting for Laurel to tell him if she was staying in Willow Valley or leaving. Staying in Willow Valley as his wife. He had to know what she was saying to Grandfather.

Ben got out of the car and closed the door quietly, telling himself that what he was about to do was wrong, not honorable, then pushing those thoughts aside and justifying his actions with the knowledge that he was desperate, falling apart by emotional inches, a breath at a time.

He went quietly forward, hesitated, then stopped outside the wooden door of the hogan and leaned close, listening.

"You must deal with your inner demons, Laurel, reach for the strength I have spoken of," Ben heard Grandfather say. "You came home to Willow Valley, but you left your heart in Virginia. Troubled, so troubled. You must free yourself of the demons of what haunts you so you may receive the love of the man who is waiting to give you his love for all time. Understand?"

"Yes, Grandfather, I understand," Laurel said. "Thank you so much. Thank you."

Ben hurried back to the patrol car and drove away, his hold on the steering wheel so tight that his knuckles turned white.

No! his mind screamed. Oh, God, no. Laurel had left her heart in Virginia? Loved a man there who was waiting to give her his love for all time? No. She had said she loved him, *him,* but now he realized what she'd meant when she had told him something had happened in Virginia to change her and that she had nothing to offer him. She loved a man back there more than she loved him. A man who was the demon who held her heart captive.

For some unknown reason she had run from that man, and Grandfather was telling her to slay the demons that had caused her to do that so she could…

No.

Ben pressed his foot on the brake and rested his forehead on the steering wheel.

He'd lost his Laurel ten years ago, he thought, a chill coursing through him, and now he'd lost her again. She would listen to Grandfather as she always had, know she must return to Virginia to solve the problems with the man who possessed her heart. The man she loved more than him.

Whatever glimmer of hope he'd had that he and Laurel were to finally have their dreams come true, live out their days together, was gone, snuffed out like a flickering flame on a candle. Gone. Forever.

Ben lifted his head, swept a hand over his tear-filled eyes, then drove on, acutely aware of the crushing weight of loneliness that consumed him.

Chapter Eleven

Three days later a single drum began to beat in a slow, steady rhythm on the reservation. The drum was joined by another, then twenty more, then more yet, until hundreds thrummed in synchronization, filling the air with the eerie, sorrowful sound. It was carried in the wind across the entire reservation and into Willow Valley.

People in town halted on the sidewalks, and shop owners came out of their stores. Everyone turned to face the rez, no one speaking, only listening to the drums.

And they knew.

The smoke had stopped rising from the center of the hogan.

Their beloved Grandfather had crossed the rainbow bridge to the other side. He had died. He was gone. Tears flowed like a river filled suddenly by the rains of the monsoon, but no one spoke because there were no words to express the chilling sense of loss.

Laurel stood in the front yard of the house she shared with her mother, tears streaming down her face, her hands wrapped around her elbows as she stared in the direction of the reservation.

Jane joined others on the sidewalk in front of the Windsong Café and pressed trembling fingertips to her lips as tears tracked her cheeks.

Dove sat on the ground outside her small house and beat the rhythm on the drum, tears splashing onto her hands.

Ben forced one foot in front of the other to reach his patrol car, then drove slowly through town, the red and blue lights on the bar flashing, the siren silent.

When he reached Grandfather's hogan, the people were gathering, staying a respectful distance away, waiting for Ben. He stood in front of the door and called Grandfather's name three times, then entered.

"Hagoonee," Ben whispered as he wrapped Grandfather in a blanket Dove had made, then lifted him into his arms. "Goodbye, Grandfather."

Ben carried his precious cargo from the hogan, the sun shining on the code-talker medallion around Grandfather's neck and laid carefully on the outside of the blanket for all to see. Cadillac approached with a wagon, followed by four elderly women who would prepare Grandfather for burial. The medallion would stay with him when he was lowered into his place in Mother Earth.

Within the next week the door of the hogan would be tightly sealed to be certain the *chendi,* the evil spirit from the dead, was kept inside.

And through the night the drums continued to beat.

The next afternoon in the far corner of the reservation, where the cemetery was located, close to two thousand people heard the farewell words of the minister of the church in Willow Valley and watched the Navajo dance of death performed to haunting chants.

Each person walked by the wooden coffin holding the still form of their beloved Grandfather, who had been dressed in the uniform he'd worn proudly as a code-talker. Each respectfully touched the medallion on his chest. Mother Earth received her gift, and the grave was filled in one handful of dirt at a time by those who wept in a long line of mourners.

The drums stopped.

The people moved slowly away with heavy hearts and tear-stained faces.

"Let's go, Laurel," Jane whispered. "It's getting very cold."

"No, you go on," Laurel said, dashing tears from her face. "I'm going to Grandfather's hogan for a while. They haven't sealed the door yet, and I'm not afraid of the *chendi*. I need to be there. I really do."

"You mustn't light a fire inside," Jane said. "It will frighten people if there is suddenly smoke coming from the hogan again."

"I won't. There are blankets there," Laurel said. "I won't stay long, Mother. I just want to say my own goodbye to Grandfather."

Jane hugged her daughter, then walked toward her car. Ben was standing about two hundred feet behind Laurel.

"Laurel is going to Grandfather's hogan for a bit, Ben," Jane said. "She needs to say goodbye in her own way, but she won't light a fire."

Ben nodded.

"Oh, how he will be missed," Jane said. "It's hard to imagine life without Grandfather." She paused. "Are you all right, Ben?"

"As well as anyone else, I guess," he said, his voice gritty. "It's a sad day for us all."

Jane nodded, patted Ben's arm and went on her

way. Ben stared at Laurel where she stood in the distance, then his shoulders slumped and he turned and walked slowly to his vehicle.

Laurel drove to Grandfather's hogan, hesitated a moment, then entered. It was surprisingly warm inside. She removed her jacket, dropped it to the ground without watching where it fell, then wrapped only one blanket around her as she sat cross-legged on the pile of blankets, looking at the cold, gray ashes in the circle in the center of the floor.

She relived her conversation with Grandfather the last time she had been here with him, heard him tell her that she must defeat the demons that held her fast after what had happened in Virginia, must reach deep within herself for strength.

"I'm trying, Grandfather," she said, fresh tears filling her eyes. "I'm trying so hard, but the demons are so strong. What if they defeat me? What if I can't win the battle?" A sob caught in her throat. "Oh, Grandfather, I'm going to miss you so much, so very, very much."

Laurel curled up on the blankets and clutched Grandfather's blanket tightly around her as she wept as though her heart was breaking into a million pieces.

Ben stood outside the hogan, his hands curling into tight fists as he heard the heartbreaking sound of Laurel's tears. He paced back and forth in front of the door, warring with himself.

Leave her alone, Skeeter, he ordered his beleaguered mind. She loved another man more than him, didn't want a future with him, wanted nothing from him, not even comfort on this day of sorrow.

But, oh, God, she sounded so sad. She was in that hogan all by herself, filled with such grief and pain over the loss of Grandfather, feeling the absence of the wise and wonderful man just as he was. She shouldn't be alone. *He* shouldn't be alone. Not now. Not now.

Ben opened the door with a trembling hand and entered the hogan. He crossed to where Laurel was huddled, dropped to one knee, then gently stroked the tears from her cheeks with his thumb.

Laurel opened her eyes and turned her head to look directly into Ben's eyes. She raised her arms to him, the blanket falling away from her. Ben took off his jacket and his Stetson and stretched out next to her, gathering her in his arms and holding her close as she cried, her face buried in his shirt.

Laurel finally quieted, drew a shuddering breath then met Ben's gaze again, his face only inches from hers. He lowered his head and kissed her gently, reverently, as though she was a fragile, wounded entity entrusted to his care.

A sob caught in Laurel's throat as she wrapped

her arms around Ben's neck, inching her fingers into his thick hair to urge his mouth harder onto hers. He hesitated, then a groan rumbled in his chest, and he delved his tongue into her mouth, meeting her tongue, as desire exploded within them.

She didn't want to think, Laurel thought frantically. She didn't want to cry. She only wanted to feel. She only wanted Ben. She was tired, so tired of attempting and failing to defeat her demons. She just wanted to savor the exquisite sensations swirling and churning within her, drink in the taste of Ben, his special aroma, the strength of his body. She loved him so much, but she had nothing to offer him but the moment. Ben. Her beloved Ben.

Laurel broke the kiss, gazed deep into Ben's eyes and saw the smoldering passion there, then moved away just far enough to shed her clothes in quick, jerky motions.

Ben frowned as he watched her.

Think, Skeeter, he ordered himself. Laurel loved another man more than she loved him. Her heart belonged to some faceless stranger in Virginia. He and Laurel would never be married, have the children they'd dreamed of so many years before, grow old together, their love strengthening with each passing year.

But, aw, damn, right now, right here, he didn't care

about any of that. He loved this woman with all that he was. He was raw with pain over the loss of Grandfather and knew that Laurel was, too. He needed to feel, not think. Make love, not weep. Live for the moment, with no thought of tomorrow. He needed Laurel.

Ben removed his clothes swiftly and reached for Laurel at the same second she reached again for him. He captured her mouth in a searing kiss, his hands skimming over her dewy skin. She pressed her body to his, flinging one leg over his as though wishing to melt into him, make them one inseparable entity. Her fingertips dug into his back, harder, then harder yet, urging him closer, wanting him...wanting him...wanting...

Ben pushed her flat onto the blanket, moved over her and into her, immediately beginning to thunder within her. It was rough and urgent, earthy and held a hint of frantic need so intense it consumed them beyond reality or reason.

The rhythm pounded, beat like the drums that had sounded for Grandfather, harder and stronger, going on and on and on. Heat coiled within them with such force it was nearly painful as they went higher and closer to the summit, then were flung over and away, not wishing to return. Their hearts raced and their breathing was labored and loud in the quiet hogan. Spasms rippled throughout them, then finally stilled.

Ben drew a ragged breath, then moved off of Laurel. Without meeting her gaze he turned and dressed as she did the same. Ben got to his feet as Laurel once again curled up on the blankets. He looked down at her for a long moment, then left the hogan.

When he stood outside in the crisp, chill air, Ben realized that from the time he'd entered the hogan, then returned to where he was standing, not one word had been spoken.

He dragged both hands down his face.

Not one word, he thought, an achy sensation gripping his throat, because there was nothing left to say.

Inside the hogan Laurel whispered Ben's name, then drifted into a strange, uneasy sleep. Images began to take shape in her mental vision, images she knew were dreams, yet she was unable to waken.

In a hazy mist she saw herself, Dove and Ben as children, sitting on the broad back of Thunder. Then the picture evolved and she was alone on the magnificent horse as a grown woman. Grandfather appeared, then they were sitting together on the ground in front of a fire, Thunder now nowhere in sight. There was just the two of them—herself and her beloved Grandfather.

"Grandfather?" she whispered. "How can you be

here? You have left us, crossed the rainbow bridge to the other side."

"I have come to you, *Dahetihhi,* my little hummingbird," Grandfather said, his voice sounding as though it was echoing from a faraway place. "I cannot finish my journey across the rainbow bridge to rest in peace because you have not completed what you must do. The demons still hold you in an iron fist."

"I can't defeat them, Grandfather," Laurel said, fresh tears filling her eyes. "I've tried, but…"

"Stop. I won't hear these words from you, *Dahetihhi,*" he said, frowning. "You are a Navajo from your father's blood. We believe that no one will ever be perfect in any endeavor they pursue. We are a humble people, yet you are placing yourself above others."

"Me? No, no, I don't believe I'm better than others. I failed, Grandfather. I told you what happened in Virginia. I wasn't good enough, and because I failed…"

"No," he said sharply. "You did not fail. You did your very best, which is the Navajo way. You were fooled by a mind quicker than yours, one that was determined to go his own way, and nothing or no one could have stopped him. You take the blame for what was not your fault.

"The demons of guilt and shame will hold you fast forever if you don't listen to me. You think you should have been able to do what no one could, be perfect, which is not the Navajo way. Do you hear me, Laurel Windsong?"

Laurel sat up straighter, a new and comforting warmth suffusing her.

"Yes," she said softly. "Yes, I finally hear you, really hear you, Grandfather. I did my best. I did. I have nothing…oh, God, I have nothing to be ashamed of.

"You're right. No one could have changed how things went, what happened. No one. Oh, Grandfather, I'm so sorry it took me so long to understand, to defeat the demons. I'm so sorry I kept you from your final journey. How can I thank you for coming to me here in what I know is a dream but yet is so real?"

"Live and love and be happy, my *Dahetihhi.* Follow your heart that has been freed at long last. I am ready now to go to the other side and rest in peace beyond the life here on Mother Earth. *Hagoonee,* Laurel."

"Goodbye, Grandfather," she said, dashing tears from her cheeks. "I'll miss you so much. Thank you for all you've done for me. I love you, Grandfather. *Hagoonee.*"

"*Ha…goo…nee,*" he said as a gray mist swirled around him and he disappeared.

More than an hour later Laurel stirred, then sat up, not certain at first where she was. She shook her head slightly to chase away the fogginess from the deep sleep, then her eyes widened.

She'd dreamed of Grandfather, she thought. He had spoken to her and she had finally, *finally,* heard the wisdom of his words.

What had happened in Virginia was not her fault.
She had defeated the demons that had held her fast.
She was free to live and love.
Love Ben.

Laurel frowned.

Ben, she thought. Had that been a dream, too? Or had Ben really entered the hogan, taken her into his arms and… They hadn't spoken, hadn't said one word aloud, but had shared lovemaking so incredibly beautiful. Had that been a dream?

Laurel shifted on the blanket, and the achy sensations in her body told her that Ben had truly come to her as she'd wept. They had reached for each other, comforted each other, made love that required that no words be spoken.

Benjamin Skeeter, she thought, a soft smile forming on her lips. The only man she had ever loved. She was free now of the ghosts of the past, could go to him with her heart filled with love for him, only him. All the hopes and dreams they'd planned on years before could now come true because of the incredible dream.

She loved Ben. Ben loved her. The future was theirs to share. Together. Forever. They were getting a second chance, could begin again.

She had to go to Ben, she thought, getting to her feet. She'd tell him, finally, of the nightmare in Virginia that had sent her running home like a frightened child. She'd tell him of the dream she'd had in the hogan and how she'd listened—and really heard—Grandfather's words and found her inner peace. Yes, she had to go to Ben. Now.

Laurel turned and picked up her jacket. Her breath caught as she saw a small rawhide pouch that had been covered by her jacket when she'd dropped it upon entering the hogan. A tiny piece of paper was pinned to the pouch.

The paper had one word written on it.
Dahetihhi.

Laurel dropped to her knees and with trembling hands, opened the pouch and tipped it toward one palm, gasping as she saw what tumbled out.

It was Grandfather's turquoise stone.

Fresh tears filled Laurel's eyes and she smiled as she curled her fingers around the precious gift.

Grandfather had left the stone for her so she would be able to gather her inner strength and courage if she faltered. He had wanted to be assured that she wouldn't fall prey again to the demons.

"Oh, Grandfather," she said, hugging the stone against her heart. "How do I thank you? You've given me so much, so very much. You've given me my life back, my freedom, my Ben." Tears filled her eyes. "Thank you. *Ahehee. Ahehee.* Thank you."

Carefully, Laurel placed the stone back in the pouch, put it in the pocket of her jacket and zipped it closed. She got to her feet, put on the jacket and went to the door. She turned and looked back, sweeping her gaze over the hogan.

The door would be sealed soon, she thought. She'd never step inside this place again, but she would never forget what had transpired here and she would be eternally grateful to the wise and wonderful man who had ended his days on Mother Earth within these walls.

"*Hagoonee,*" she said. "Goodbye, my Grandfather. Rest in peace."

A chill wind whipped against Laurel when she left the hogan. The sky was gray with approaching rain and the curtain of the darkness of night waiting to fall. She hurried to her van and drove away from the hogan, only to stop before she'd gone very far.

As much as she wanted to see Ben, she thought, she should wait until tomorrow. She was exhausted and emotionally drained, despite her nap in the hogan. She had so much to tell Ben, explain to him, and she needed to be strong, not end up a weepy mess unable to make sense of all she needed to say. Yes, she'd wait until tomorrow.

Laurel pressed on the gas pedal and drove slowly on. When she passed Dove's house, she was tempted to stop, but resisted the urge to finally tell her best friend what had happened in Virginia.

And when she got home, she decided, she would somehow not reveal to her mother what had happened in the hogan, would not show her mother Grandfather's gift of the turquoise stone. No, Ben must be the first to learn of all that had taken place. That was the way it should—and would—be done.

When Laurel entered the house, Jane got quickly to her feet.

"Oh, heavens, I've been so worried about you, Laurel," she said. "You were gone so long. Are you all right, sweetheart?"

Laurel rested her hand lightly on the pocket of the jacket where the soft pouch was nestled.

"Yes," she said, smiling. "I'm fine. I'm sorry if you were concerned, Mother. I lost track of time, but, oh, Mom, I'm more than fine. I'm at peace at long last. What happened in Virginia wasn't my fault. I understand that now because Grandfather... Well, let's just say I finally heard what I couldn't hear before."

"Darling, that's wonderful," Jane said, hugging Laurel. She moved back to look into her daughter's eyes. "Yes, the ghosts are gone. Your eyes are bright and sparkling. I'm so happy for you."

Laurel laughed. "And I'm so hungry. Have you eaten dinner yet?"

"No, I was waiting for you, doing my worried-mother thing that requires that I lose my appetite," Jane said, smiling. "But now that you're home and have such glorious news, I'm starving. Go wash up, then let's make omelets and toss all kinds of goodies into them, everything we can find in the refrigerator. And we'll have buttery toast and hot chocolate and..."

Jane was still listing the menu for dinner as she disappeared into the kitchen. Laurel went into her bedroom and hung her jacket in the closet. She removed the pouch from the pocket and sat down on the edge of the bed, opening it with gentle care, to assure herself that the stone was really there. She stroked the beautiful blue turquoise with one finger-tip, a peaceful smile forming on her lips.

"Laurel," Jane called in the distance. "Are you coming, honey?"

"Yes, I'll be right there, Mother. I just need to wash my hands."

Laurel placed the pouch in the small drawer of the nightstand next to the bed.

Tomorrow, she thought, getting to her feet. Tomorrow she would go to Ben and tell him everything. She would count down the hours until tomorrow.

Chapter Twelve

Laurel slept late the next morning and woke feeling well rested. She showered and dressed in jeans and a bright blue sweater, acutely aware of her sense of anticipation about seeing Ben.

She also knew that the comforting warmth that was deep within her was the inner peace she now possessed regarding what had transpired in Virginia due to the dream about Grandfather in the hogan.

She removed the precious pouch from the nightstand drawer, zipped it into the pocket of her red jacket, which she left hanging in the closet, then went into the kitchen for something to eat.

A note on the table from her mother informed Laurel that Jane had gone to early church, then was heading out to the rez to pick apples with May for cobbler to serve at the café.

"Okay," Laurel said, then fixed herself some toast and coffee.

After cleaning up following her meal, Laurel stared at the telephone on the kitchen wall, drew a steadying breath, then lifted the receiver and punched in the numbers for Ben's house. When the answering machine clicked on, she hung up without leaving a message.

Next she called the sheriff's office and was greeted by a cheerful Bobby.

"Nope, it's his day off, Laurel," Bobby said. "He's going to ride Thunder for a while, then do some fishing on the far side of the rez. He has his hand radio with him, but he told me not to bother him unless it was a real emergency." He paused. "Do you need to talk to him about a real emergency?"

Yes, Bobby, Laurel mentally yelled. She was finally ready to tell Ben everything she had been keeping from him, the secrets within her that had stood between them. She wanted to see him, touch him, kiss him, declare her love for him over and over and make sweet, slow love with him for hours.

She wanted to talk with him about their future life

together, the babies they would have and... Yes, this was an emergency. Ten years had already been lost, and that was far, far too many.

"No, it's not an emergency, Bobby," she said quietly. "I'll catch up with him later."

"Any message?"

"No, thank you, that won't be necessary. Have a nice day, Bobby." Laurel replaced the receiver. "Darn."

Three hours later she was so tired of pacing back and forth across the small living room that she called Ben's house again and left a message on his machine, asking him to telephone her when he arrived home, her pride not allowing her to drive from one end of the rez to the other to look for him.

At ten o'clock that night Laurel went to bed, having heard nothing from Benjamin Skeeter.

The next day Laurel repeated her call to Ben's house, then to the office. Bobby informed her that Ben was in court in Prescott for the day, dealing with a DWI charge against one of the guys from the rez.

"Any message, Laurel?" Bobby said.

"No, thank you, Bobby, but... No," she said, then sighed as she hung up the receiver.

She left another request on Ben's answering machine to call her, but bedtime came with the telephone in the Windsong home being silent the entire evening.

* * *

On Tuesday morning Laurel asked her mother to please call her from the café if Ben came in for lunch.

"Oh?" Jane said, slipping on her coat. "Well, sure, all right. And then what?"

"I'll come down there, because I need to speak to him," Laurel said, not looking directly at her mother.

"I see. It must be important."

"Mmm."

"Should I tell him you're on your way?" Jane said, raising her eyebrows.

"That's not necessary," Laurel said. "Just let me know if he's there. Have any clothes you want washed?"

Jane laughed. "That's the line that means mind my own business. Bye, sweetheart."

"*Hagoonee,*" Laurel said dismally.

The delay in being able to talk to Ben, Laurel admitted to herself after her mother left the house, had caused her to become a nervous wreck. The wonderful sense of anticipation had changed into a bevy of butterflies that had taken up residency in her stomach.

Shortly after one o'clock Jane called from the café to say that Ben had just arrived and ordered a lunch of chili and corn bread.

"I don't need to know what he's going to eat," Laurel said sharply. "I... Oh, Mother, I'm sorry. I shouldn't have snapped at you. My nerves are just a tad... I'm sorry."

"You're forgiven," Jane said, smiling. "And you don't need to tell me how tense you are, Laurel. I live with you, remember? You're like a clock that's being wound tighter and tighter over the past few days."

"Oh."

"Well, hop in your pretty red van and zip down here before Ben gets away," Jane said. "Our carpet can't stand much more of your pacing."

"Oh. Well. I didn't realize that you were aware that I... Forget it," Laurel said, rolling her eyes. "Nothing gets past you because you're a mother."

"Exactly. Ta-ta."

Laurel hung up the receiver, pressed one hand on her butterfly-filled stomach then rushed to her room for her jacket. She checked the pocket to be certain that the pouch with the beautiful stone was still safely there, then left the house.

Outside the Windsong Café Laurel hesitated, gathered her courage, told herself to forget her misplaced pride, then entered. She slid into the bench seat opposite Ben in the booth where he was buttering a piece of corn bread, the cast on his hand causing him no problems with the process.

"Hello, Ben," she said quietly, unable to produce a smile.

"Laurel," he said, glancing up at her with no readable expression on his face.

She folded her hands in her lap, then lifted her chin.

"You haven't returned my calls," she said.

"No, I haven't," he said, then took a bite of the corn bread.

"Why?"

Ben chewed and swallowed, then looked directly at her.

"Because I don't think we have anything to discuss, Laurel. There were things on the table for a while, like the prospect of us continuing to see each other, but that's no longer an option, so…" He shrugged.

"I don't understand," she said, feeling the color drain from her face.

Ben leaned slightly forward. "We have nothing to discuss. Is that clear enough for you? Are we *communicating* here? If you'll excuse me, Laurel, I'd like to finish my lunch. Okay?"

"Yes, of course, I…" Laurel said, her voice trembling.

But then she stopped and splayed her hand on the pocket of her jacket where Grandfather's stone was nestled.

"No, it's not okay, Benjamin Skeeter," she said, her eyes flashing. "I want to talk to you. I intend to talk to

you. Nothing is going to keep me from talking to you.
I'd prefer to have that conversation in private, and I
will. Therefore, be at your house at seven o'clock this
evening. Be there. *Is that clear enough for you?*"

Ben opened his mouth to retort, then realized he
was so stunned by Laurel's outburst that nothing was
going to come out, and snapped his mouth closed
again. He nodded jerkily as he stared at her.

"Fine," she said, then slid from the booth and
hurried out of the café.

Ben looked up to see a dozen pairs of eyes riveted
on him, then hunched over his bowl and shoveled in
a spoonful of chili.

That evening, after a dinner Laurel had taken four
bites of while ignoring the amused expression on her
mother's face, she dressed in gray slacks and a soft
cranberry-colored sweater.

This had been, she thought as she brushed her
hair, one of the longest afternoons of her entire life.
How had it come to this? Her entire future happiness
depended on what took place at Ben's house tonight.
If he refused to listen to her, to really hear what she
was saying, then... No. She couldn't bear the
thought of that. She just couldn't.

She reached behind her head to begin to braid her
hair, then hesitated.

She'd allow her hair to fall free as a tangible reminder that *she* was now free of her demons. A silly idea, she supposed, but she needed all the courage she could muster from any source available.

"This is it," she said to her reflection in the mirror over the dresser. "This is really and truly it."

When Laurel entered the living room, her mother looked up from where she was sitting on the sofa watching the news and smiled.

"You look lovely, Laurel," Jane said. "Your hair is so pretty like that, just gorgeous." She paused. "I hope things go well when you see Ben."

"I guess it was easy to figure out that that's where I'm going," Laurel said. "I just hope I'm not too late to make him believe how very much I love him. Just talking about it makes the butterflies start their zooming thing in my stomach again. Well, I'm off. Wish me luck."

"I wish you love," Jane said.

Laurel smiled and nodded, then slipped her jacket on, her hand automatically sliding across the pocket holding the pouch.

"Bye," she said, starting toward the door.

"Ta-ta," Jane said, looking at the television again. "Hopefully, you won't be back until tomorrow."

"Mother!" Laurel stopped in her tracks, a warm flush staining her cheeks.

"Ta-ta," Jane said again, waggling the fingers of one hand in the air.

Laurel left the house and drove slowly toward Ben's home.

Ben placed the screen in front of the fire he had started in the living room hearth. He turned as he heard a vehicle approaching the house.

Laurel was here, he thought. The hours since she'd told him in no uncertain terms that she was going to speak to him, like it or not, had seemed like an eternity. Man, what a long afternoon.

Aw, hell, didn't she get it? There was nothing left to say. Yeah, sure, she'd declared her love for him. Big deal. What she'd failed to mention was that there was some guy in Virginia she loved even more. Was he going to have to stand here and listen to her tell him that? No way. He'd—

Ben jerked as a knock sounded, then strode across the room and opened the front door.

"Hello, Ben," Laurel said.

"Yeah," he said, frowning. "Come in."

She wasn't playing fair, he thought as he closed the door behind Laurel. She'd left her hair free of the braid, and his fingers were already tingling, wanting to sift through that ebony waterfall and... Skeeter, get a grip.

"A fire in the hearth," Laurel said. "How nice May I take off my jacket?"

"What?" Ben said. "Oh. Sure."

Laurel placed her jacket on a chair, then sat down in another chair that faced the fire. Ben walked forward slowly and slouched onto the opposite one.

"Let's cut to the chase, shall we?" he said, frowning. "Why are you here? What is it you want to talk to me about, Laurel?"

"You're not going to make this easy for me, are you?" she said, clutching her hands tightly in her lap.

Ben lifted one shoulder in a shrug, then laced his hands loosely on his chest as he crossed his legs at the ankle.

"Ben," Laurel said, then drew a steadying breath. "I love you. I'm deeply in love with you, but.. "

"Cut," he said, slicing one hand through the air. "Let me fill in the blanks. You love me but, gosh, Ben, there's this guy in Virginia I love more than I love you. That's the way it is, Skeeter, and I thought I should clear that up. The end."

"What are you talking about?" Laurel said, confused.

"Oh, come on, Laurel," Ben said, pushing himself upward in the chair. "I was outside Grandfather's hogan and heard the bit about your heart being in Virginia. I don't need to be hit by a brick, lady.

"And as far as what happened between us after Grandfather's funeral? The lovemaking we shared in his hogan? Maybe it was wrong, I don't know. We needed comfort, a momentary escape from the sorrow of losing a man who was like no other. I'm not sorry about what we did, but if you are, go for it.

"The big secret you've been keeping about why you came running home is clear as a bell now," he continued. "You had a romance go sour in Virginia, you still love the jerk and you have to decide whether to go back and try to patch things up. How am I doing? I'd say I'm right on the money."

Laurel narrowed her eyes, slid a quick glance at the pocket of her jacket where it lay on the chair, then crossed her arms over her breasts.

"You are so wrong it's a crime, Benjamin Skeeter, and you should arrest yourself," she said. "There is no man in Virginia. There has been no one in my life of any importance since I left here ten years ago. I told you that and it was the truth. You've got a lot of nerve listening to a private conversation between me and Grandfather, but I'll let that part pass."

"Mmm," Ben said, frowning.

Laurel sighed and dropped her hands back to her lap.

"Ben," she said quietly, "I need to know you're going to listen to me, really hear what I'm about to tell you. We destroyed our entire future together years ago because we didn't really hear what the other was saying. This is our chance to have our forever again, but it won't happen if you don't hear my words, listen with an open mind and heart. Will you do that? Please?"

Ben shifted his gaze to the leaping flames in the hearth for a long moment, then met Laurel's gaze again.

"Yeah," he said, nodding. "Yes, I will."

"Thank you. Ben, you misunderstood what you heard when you were outside Grandfather's hogan. He said my heart was in Virginia, but it was because it was being held by the demons of what happened there. He said that until I defeated those demons, I wouldn't be able to live and love—love you—the way that I should, the way that I want to.

"I tried so hard to fight the ghosts, the demons," she said, struggling against threatening tears, "but I wasn't strong enough. I was losing the battle. Losing myself. Losing you."

"Wait a minute," Ben said, shaking his head. "Let's back up here. If the big secret isn't a man in Virginia, then what exactly happened back there? What created these demons you're speaking of and sent you running home?"

"Okay," Laurel said, her voice not quite steady. "Oh, God, this is so hard for me to… All right. I worked as a counselor, a psychologist, at an exclusive year-round boarding school for high school students from very affluent families.

"Some of them were there because their parents were so career oriented they didn't have time for them. Others had gotten into trouble with the law because they were bored little rich kids. Some were simply decent young people obtaining an excellent education."

Ben nodded, his gaze riveted on Laurel.

"I, of course," she continued, "dealt with the ones who had problems. There was a boy, David, sixteen years old, who was expelled from three public high schools for breaking the rules. When he was fifteen, he attempted suicide, which was chalked up to an attempt to gain his parents' attention.

"His mother and father were divorced, and the sad thing was neither one of them wanted the responsibility of having custody of their son who was in such emotional turmoil. So they put him in that boarding school where I was working."

"Nice people," Ben said with a snort of disgust.

"David began to act out at the school, cutting classes, being late for curfew, all kinds of things. Then his roommate told one of the teachers that David had spoken of killing himself and that he'd make sure he did it right this time. The teacher immediately referred David to me."

Ben nodded.

"I spent hours with him, Ben," Laurel said. "Weeks into months. He slowly opened up, revealed how lonely he was, how unwanted and unloved he felt by his mother and father. He was angry and hurt, an unhappy child. So unhappy.

"David was brilliant, and I centered on that, telling him how he could create a world for himself wherever he wanted, be whatever he wanted to be. I focused on his worth, how much he had to offer, how he had to believe in himself even though the two most important people in his life had forsaken him.

"Suicide wasn't the answer, I told him, living was. He could rise above the pain, the hurt, the disappointments and betrayals, and show the world what he could do, how fine a man he could become."

"Yeah," Ben said. "That's good. Yeah."

"David began to buckle down and study, was getting top grades in his classes, following all the rules of the school, doing everything right. He began to smile, laugh right out loud sometimes when we were having a counseling session. He talked about a future as an attorney who specialized in family law, one who represented the children of divorce, made certain they didn't get lost in the legal shuffle.

"I was thrilled with what I was seeing in David.

All my training was paying off. I had actually reached him, gotten through to him and…"

Laurel stopped speaking, pressed her lips tightly together and shook her head.

Ben leaned forward to rest his elbows on his knees and laced his fingers together.

"And what?" he said.

"It…it was all an act on David's part," Laurel said, her eyes filling with tears. "All of it. Those weeks and months were a game he was playing just because it was something to do. I fell for it, Ben. I missed every signal he sent out that it was a phony performance because I was too busy patting myself on the back for doing such a terrific job of getting David on the right track."

"What happened?" Ben said quietly.

"He…David…he killed himself. He hung himself in the closet in his room at the school. His roommate found him and… Oh, God, Ben, I couldn't believe it. I was so certain that… I lost all confidence in myself, blamed myself for David's death, fell prey to the demons of guilt and shame and came running home to Willow Valley."

"Aw, Laurel," Ben said. "I'm so sorry this happened to you. Did he—did David leave a note?"

Two tears slid down Laurel's cheeks and she wiped them away with her fingertips.

"Oh, yes," Laurel said, a slight edge to her voice.

"He wanted to be certain that it was understood that he was the one in charge. The note said *I win*. The game was over, he was tired of it and, as far as he was concerned, he'd won."

"Man," Ben said, dragging one hand down his face.

"I couldn't talk about it," Laurel said. "I couldn't bear to tell anyone. Not even Dove. Not you. I told my mother, of course, and she finally convinced me to talk to Grandfather even though he was ill. She said that he would want me to come to him with this."

"Of course he would," Ben said.

"That's what you overheard, Ben, about my heart being in Virginia. My heart, my mind, my very soul, was being held captive there by the demons of what I perceived to be my terrible failure that cost a young man his life."

"It wasn't your fault," Ben said, straightening in the chair again. "David obviously had a plan he'd put in motion. It's clear to me that nothing could have stopped him, Laurel. Nothing. No one. Grandfather would have understood that. David chose to end his days on his own terms, just as Grandfather did."

Laurel nodded. "That's what Grandfather told me, urged me to realize, believe, but I was still struggling with it when he died.

"But I'm getting ahead of myself here. When I went to see Grandfather to talk to him about my troubles, he asked me if I was afraid of the *chendi* and I said no. He suggested, strongly suggested, really, that I might want to come to the hogan after he was gone because there was peace to be found there."

"And you went to the hogan after the funeral," Ben said.

"Yes. On the day Grandfather and I spoke he showed me a beautiful deep blue turquoise stone, Ben. His mother had given it to him when he was leaving for the war. It wasn't magical, he said, it was meant to make him stop and reach within himself for strength and courage. He said I had more inner strength than I realized.

"After the funeral, when you came to the hogan and we…we made love, I slept after you left. I had strange dreams, one tumbling into the next. Then I saw Grandfather and he spoke to me in the dream about defeating the ghosts, the demons. When I woke, I knew I was finally free, that I had really heard what Grandfather was saying."

"Thank God for that," Ben said.

"Yes. At long last, after so many months, so many tears, I finally understood that David's death wasn't my fault. I was free, thanks to Grandfather, of the demons. Free to live. Free to love. You. To love you,

Ben. I just hope and pray that I'm not too late, that I haven't destroyed everything between us."

"No, oh, no, you're not too late," Ben said, getting to his feet. "I love you, Laurel. I was so ripped up when I thought you were in love with some guy in Virginia. Thank God you had that dream about Grandfather that day in the hogan."

"I know. But there's more, Ben," she said, rising to stand in front of him. "When I picked up my jacket to leave the hogan, I realized that Grandfather had left me a gift that I hadn't seen when I first came into the hogan and had covered it with my coat. Let me show you."

Laurel retrieved the soft rawhide pouch from the pocket of her jacket and handed it to Ben.

"What is it?" he said.

"Open it. It's one of Grandfather's most treasured possessions, and he gave it to me."

Ben eased the top of the small pouch apart and tipped it into his hand, his eyes widening as he saw what tumbled into his palm.

"My God, Laurel, it's the turquoise stone Grandfather's mother gave him. What an incredible gift this is."

"I know that. I believe he wanted me to have it so I'd remember to reach for my inner strength as the future unfolds with all it will bring. I want us to share this precious stone, Ben. Grandfather loved *us,*" she said, tears echoing in her voice. "He couldn't bear the thought that my demons were going to keep us apart, keep us from fulfilling our dreams together."

Laurel took a shuddering breath and lifted her chin. "Benjamin Skeeter, will you marry me? Will you be my life's partner until death parts us, then beyond? Will you be the father of our children? Will you share with me all the dreams we had so many years ago?"

Ben laid the pouch on the flagstones fronting the fireplace, then carefully placed the turquoise stone on top of it. He turned, closed the distance between him and Laurel and framed her face in his hands.

"Laurel Windsong, I would be honored to be your husband," he said, making no attempt to hide the tears glistening in his eyes. "I've waited so long for you, and now you're home, really home, with me. We'll tell our children about Grandfather and the great gift he gave us. Our future together."

"Yes," Laurel said, smiling at the same time that tears filled her eyes. "Our children will grow up here in Willow Valley, just as we did.

"I believe in myself again, too, and know I can help those who are troubled. Kids like Yazzie who are so weary of being poor, having so little, yet not knowing how to change how things are. I'll reach out to them and make a difference in their lives. Oh, Ben, I love you so much."

Ben lowered his head and kissed his future wife with a gentle reverence that brought fresh tears to both of their eyes. Then the kiss intensified and passion flared like the leaping flames in the hearth. They sank to the plush Navajo rug and in the glow of the firelight made love that sealed their commitment to their future. To their forever again. And then they slept with visions of all they would have in the years ahead as all their dreams came true.

Later, Ben stirred, then shifted up on one forearm to look at the embers in the hearth. His breath caught. He whispered Laurel's name until she opened her eyes.

"Laurel," he said, awe ringing in his voice. "Look. Look at the stone."

She pushed herself upward, and Ben sat up behind her as they stared at the pouch he'd laid on the flagstones.

The stone seemed to be glowing brightly from within, causing the beautiful blue color to shimmer in the firelight. Then, slowly, the glow dimmed and the stone was as it had been.

Laurel tilted her head back to smile up at Ben.

"Grandfather is at peace now," she said. "He's completed his journey across the rainbow bridge."

She looked at the stone again. "*Ahehee,* wise warrior, our Grandfather. Thank you."

"*Ahehee,*" Ben whispered. "For all and everything and more."

Epilogue

Laurel Windsong and Benjamin Skeeter were united in marriage in a candlelight service held in the church in Willow Valley on Christmas Eve.

Laurel wore an exquisite white, intricately beaded deerskin dress that had belonged to her father's mother. Ben wore a black Western-cut suit with a crisp white shirt and a rawhide bolo tie.

Determined that she and Ben should share Grand-father's gift of the turquoise stone, Laurel and Ben met with their lifelong friend on the reservation, Charlie Streamwalker, who made jewelry to sell in the shops in Willow Valley.

Charlie and his wife designed and made matching sterling silver wedding bands for the couple, then carefully mounted four chips of turquoise from Grandfather's stone on the top of each ring.

The remainder of the stone was crafted into a lovely teardrop hanging from a silver chain for Laurel, and the last chunky piece was on a silver disk that created Ben's bolo tie.

A beaming Cadillac was given the assignment of letting everyone in town and on the rez know that a huge barbecue to celebrate the long-awaited wedding would be held on the reservation in the spring when the weather once again turned warm.

Dove was Laurel's maid of honor and Doc Willie was Ben's best man. Jane Windsong smiled through her tears as she listened to Laurel and Ben exchange vows that she knew they would honor until death parted them and even beyond, when it was time to cross the rainbow bridge.

"Our baby is happy at last, Jimmy," Jane whispered, dashing a tear from her cheek.

"You may kiss your bride," the minister said finally.

Ben framed Laurel's face in his hands and kissed her softly, tenderly and so reverently.

"I love you, Mrs. Skeeter," he said, his voice gritty with emotion.

"And I love you, Mr. Skeeter," Laurel said, tears

of joy shimmering in her eyes. "This is the first moment of our forever."

"Again," Ben said.

* * * * *

HOTEL
MARCHAND

**Four sisters.
A family legacy.
And someone is out to destroy it.**

**A captivating new limited
continuity, launching June 2006**

The most beautiful hotel in New Orleans,
and someone is out to destroy it. But mystery,
danger and some surprising family revelations
and discoveries won't stop the Marchand sisters
from protecting their birthright…
and finding love along the way.

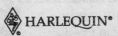

**Hidden in the secrets of antiquity,
lies the unimagined truth...**

Introducing

ROGUE
Angel™

a brand-new line filled with mystery
and suspense, action and adventure,
and a fascinating look into history.

And it all begins with DESTINY.

In a sealed crypt in
France, where the
terrifying legend of
the beast of Gevaudan
begins to unravel,
Annja Creed discovers
a stunning artifact
that will seal her destiny.

*Available every other
month starting
July 2006, wherever
you buy books.*

GRA1

COMING NEXT MONTH